The Road Home
Finding My Way

An American woman's journey
through grief, peril, romance and
rediscovery in South Africa

Barbara Lukavsky

Debbie
Enjoy the read
Love Life & Love
Barbara Lukavsky

Published by Ah! Plause! Productions

Cover Design: Tim Blumer

To Grant and Shannon
and their dad who loved them so much

My Thanks

I've learned that life can change with the tick of the clock and I want the people I love, my family and friends, to always know they are important. You are the angels who appear in different forms and surround me. I'm grateful for that.

I'm thankful for my big brother, Dick, who has always been there to lead the way and his wife, Cindy...my sister, Marty (without her I couldn't have told this story)...my younger brother, Jerry, who is sensitive when I need it most and his wife, Fran...and their families, my nieces and nephews.

I'm thankful for Tania, my daughter-in-law and loving mother to my grandchildren, Grant and Shannon who keep me in their lives...Shelley and Tracy who still share their lives with me years after their dad's death...and their seven children.

I'm thankful for the colorful people in my life who became characters in this book...and to wonderful friends who encouraged me to tell this story and to those who supported me while I was living it...Sunnie and Roger for who they are...Larry and Gloria for history...Jeramy and Chuck who are steady and constant...Joyce and Rick and Mary and Kay, solid friends who include me in their lives...Pat and Cecil for their unending loyalty...Art who gave me a shoulder to cry on and Jim Davis who did the same.

I'm thankful for Byron who joined me while there were still miles to go on life's journey. He has stayed beside me to pull me back from the dark place. He has given me the courage to tell my story and he gave me the strength to fully mourn. He helps me honor the life I had before and build a life today.

I love you all.

Special Thanks To

Tim Blumer
the artist who felt the heart of this story
and turned it into a beautiful book cover

Ah! Plause! productions and The Covington Group
for printing and publishing

United States Lighthouse Society
for the cover photo

I hold it true, whate'er befall;
I feel it, when I sorrow most;
'Tis better to have loved and lost
Than never to have loved at all.

—Alfred Lord Tennyson 1850

~ 1 ~

Leaving South Africa

I move through the line of passengers boarding American Airlines for the sixteen-hour flight home. The bullet hole above my knee cap pulses and feels swollen as it will for years to come. In my luggage, a purse is blood-stained and wrapped in clippings from a Johannesburg newspaper. In English and in Afrikaan, headlines read: Lucky to be Alive!

The photographer had captured me at my thinnest. I'd probably lost twenty pounds and two sizes by then. Beneath the photo, the captions read:

Tour guide Magiel Fedrick of Pretoria and American businesswoman, Barbara Lukavsky of Des Moines, Iowa, were shot in a hijacking on the road to Empangeni. They are lucky to be alive.

The reporter scribbled details for his follow-up story while I kept vigil at Frik's bedside in the medical centre at Empangeni, a few miles outside of Durban. Frik's wounds were more serious than mine as he took three

~

bullets. He had protected me, covered me with his body, not just during the hijacking but during those desperate days of my life. Now, I go home.

Frik drove me to Johannesburg International in a Jeep-type truck used for the family landscaping business. It is late afternoon on a clear, eighty-degree day at the end of February, summer in South Africa.

Once inside, we take seats at a small corner table in the cafe. The airport is huge, sophisticated and modern as a luxurious hotel built of steel, chrome, tile and glass--cold materials, except for indirect lighting and sunlight. Windows look out over the runway and I am reminded their sky is not a brilliant sea blue as in America, but a pale, calming blue that looks soft as a baby's blanket. I remember seeing flags flapping at the entrance to the airport--the central flag with its bands of chili red, blue, green, yellow and strips of black and white, all symbolizing The Republic of South Africa, a diverse, post-Mandela democracy. They call it a Rainbow Nation.

Tourists, families and natives, predominantly black, are everywhere. Professional women and tourists have dressed like me, casually in jeans and boot-shoes. I wear a black wrap over my blouse because it will be cool on the plane. No diamonds or jewels. It's not safe. Tribal women are wrapped in colorful kaftans and elaborate headdresses to honor their traditions, however ancient those traditions might be. In this hustle-bustle of the crowded airport, why do I feel so alone?

I am anxious. I am sad and unsure. What will happen in the future? Is it true, you can't go home again? Who waits for me? Nobody. No one.

My son, my only child, is dead. My husband is dead. On Christmas Day, my late son's wife took my grand-children and moved twelve-hundred miles away and left everything that was my son's life behind.

I look at Frik and he is very handsome, though he seems angry with me. I know a separation or situation is happening between us. He has started to pull in a different direction. I am aware of that. I know it needs to happen. I know that is the case and the way things have to move. There is tension between us. I feel antag-onism coming from him. His tone sounds harsh and his voice shows frustration. He's abrupt, almost hos-tile. Frustrated, I think, because his life has been dis-rupted. I am leaving and he is not coming with me to America, as he had dreamed. The conversation I remember is this:

"Sometimes it's easier to be angry than to say what you feel," I say. "Let's not do this...be unpleasant. It's inappropriate for where we are." I put my hand on his and say, "We had a good run."

He settles down and we order cups of Rooibos—five roses—tea. It is said in South Africa, have a cup of Rooibos—it will take care of anything. If you're sick, have a cup of Rooibos. If you're depressed, have a cup of Rooibos. If you're sad, Rooibos. The taste is mild, caffeine-free, earthy and slightly sweet. What I need.

"I know how to take a relationship and put it in a box and put it up on a shelf," Frik says. "You can take the box down once in awhile and look at it but you live your life without looking in the box."

I think, *he's telling me that about me...how he'll deal with me.*

Why is he staying here with me? I ask myself. Why is he waiting? I know he is moving on and going back to his old girlfriend and had talked to her in the last couple days. Why doesn't he leave? I wonder. But I appreciate that he stays. He waits with me for two hours. We read and talk. We talk about his two schoolboy sons I had learned to love dearly. We talk about his family, his parents and brothers who had taken me in as if I belonged to them. I feel I am leaving a new family. I am leaving them all and I loved them and they loved me.

Then I am in line, moving slowly toward the boarding gate and I am thinking. I had never believed there was anything I could not do or face. I used to say I've faced enough in life that I don't think there is much that could derail me. The only thing that could would be the loss of my child.

Scottie's death did derail me and I am sure I hadn't faced it. Then Gene died, too.

I watch Frik walk away. I stand in line and see him turn a corner and disappear. Then I see him lean back around the corner and look at me and mouth, "Are you okay?"

I say, "Yes."

He turns the corner again. I watch over the railing as I board...to see his image, that head of hair, that mustache, those shoulders, but he is not there.

* * *

Nine years later, I am here. Home. A world away from South Africa. At Breakfast Club with my friends --Senator Kramer, Sunnie, Jeramy, Kay and Connie are in the group--I am able to talk to them about Scottie, Gene and Frik. My friends say, "Write it. You lived it. You need to write it."

I start to question whether or not I will--or should-- tell the story.

I have decided to try.

~ 2 ~

The Trip

"We'd like you to go on this trip with us, Barb," Matt Rosen said. "You and Gene had talked about going to South Africa and we want you with us."

"I can't, Matt," I said. "I can't."

"Yes, you can. We'll look after you."

Matt was director of the Des Moines Botanical Center and had organized the trip for members, our friends. He called to say there was room for me.

"Everything is different now," I said.

There were mostly couples taking the trip and being with couples made me feel more alone, reminding me of what I didn't have. I avoided the couples Gene and I had known and turned down most invitations.

"You won't be alone, Barb," Matt said "Billie Ray's going without Robert. Dawn Taylor's going without Jack. You'll be with us."

Why am I staying here? I wondered. Scottie had been gone for six months and Gene for two. Gene's daughter, Shelley, encouraged me to go.

"Dad wanted to take you on a safari," Shelley said. "He always talked about it and he didn't get to go. That's why you should. You can. It'll be a pleasant trip. You need to do it."

Our relationship, Shelley's and mine, had become comfortable. She had started working in one of my stores two years before her dad died and working together gave us our own relationship that was better than stepmother, stepdaughter. We were business associates and friends. Besides Shelley, everyone I asked said, go.

"Live your life, Barbie," Gene said before he died. He made me promise. When I was debating, I knew he would have wanted me to accomplish what he couldn't. And I felt travel might free me from my sadness. I'd find another culture and though I'd want to share it with the people I had lost, it would help remove me from what was left of the day-to-day. It could take me away from the pain.

Matt and Kay Rosen have always been good to me. I'll be in a safe place with them, I thought. And I wasn't in a good place by myself. How could I be?

I called Matt and told him I'd changed my mind. I'd decided to go.

There were twenty in the group. Traveling coach is not conducive to good sleep so we all took a little something, like an aspirin or a sleeping sedative to help us relax. The flight was uneventful and didn't seem too long. We landed in Iceland to refuel and soon after, the stewardess woke us for a final serving of breakfast. I felt like I had companionship on the flight. The ladies in the group made an effort to look after me...did you bring your Calamine Lotion? And snacks? You'll need snacks. And I know you got your shots.

A portly, little man who seemed old and seasoned, like he had come with the territory, met us at the airport when we landed. He drove a small bus and spoke to us with his Afrikaan accent.

"Welcome to South Africa," he said in a way that sounded like his words were clipped and yet, musical. "I am your today's guide, Raymond."

I loved hearing his accent. It was melodic and rhythmic. It was pretty to listen to, though my ear wasn't tuned to it and I didn't understand everything he said. He was a pleasant man with a big belly and sort of a bulbous nose. He drove us around the first day and in his heavy accent, he told us about the history of his country. He took us to the Capital city of Pretoria to see Voortrekker Monument that honors the "fore-trekkers," Dutch emigrants of the early 1800s. At Parliament and Church Square people strolled and bicycled and clicked cameras to get shots of the massive stone buildings designed in a semi-circle, with east and west wings spread wide, like giant arms.

The walkway leading to and from the sites was a colonnade surrounded by Jacaranda trees with their dark, leafy green leaves. The setting was beautiful, yet the landscape seemed stark, not as soft and lush as where I was raised in the Midwest. It was hot and ladies carried little hand-held fans. I was impressed with the activity, the native landscape, buildings and grounds.

I had thought we'd be going into the wild. I hadn't expected so much sophistication, so much beauty. There would be no question that South Africa is a harder country, especially out on the road, I'd come to learn. Already, the early experience of that first day had begun to change the perspective of a white woman from Iowa. Out of forty-two million South Africans, twelve million are white. I was a minority in a black culture. I'd never known that feeling before.

I looked around, trying to take in the sensations of a culture and a world I did not know. What was expected of me? It piqued my awareness. It stimulated me. In time, I would learn to be a visitor, a comfortable guest.

"Oom Paul," Raymond said, returning us to the tour. He led our group to the statue of a figure in formal top coat and top hat. It was Paul Kruger, Fifth

President of the Republic of South Africa, standing center stage on the square. "The face of resistance against the British in the Second Boer War. Look at his face on the Krugerrand," Raymond said. "They laid his body there," he pointed. "There in the Heroes Acre."

Raymond, our jolly, little welcome party of one, became one of many fascinations on the first day of our stay. It was late afternoon when a clock the size of Big Ben chimed from one of two towers in the government complex and we moved on. We stopped in Johannesburg and strolled through an open market place, drawn to the comings and goings, tasting samples of food, fascinated by the native dress--the wraps, jeweled necklaces and huge earrings, the raw goods and handcrafted souvenirs. Carvings, textiles, beads. All beautiful.

"We want you to stay with us," I told Raymond when he returned us to our lodging, a small bed and breakfast. "We like you! We love your accent!"

"If you think I have an accent," he said, "wait 'til you hear the young man who's joining us," And in came Frik to be our next driver.

Frik was six feet-seven inches tall and at first I thought he was long and gawky, but he was charming and nice and he spoke in that wonderful accent.

It was dark by the time Frik drove us to dinner at a restaurant outside of Johannesburg. I noticed small streetlights along the road, tall poles with a single

∽

globe, not modern, but quaint like the street lamps along the lakeshore in the town where I had grown up. We drove what seemed like a long way and I realized we had made several U-turns and I wondered, does this guy know where he's going?

I remember that night so well.

I had tried to convince myself I was stable and strong, but a feeling of being alone overwhelmed me during dinner. I had nobody and I was with no one. My life had been built around certain beliefs and connections that were no longer there. I had thought I knew what life was supposed to be, but it had become a mystery. I couldn't make any sense of it. I don't know why the good Lord thought I should have to handle this grief in my lifetime. What had I done that was so bad that I should have to go on without my only child and my husband. I found no answer.

I left dinner in tears. I didn't want to make a scene and ruin the evening and affect the mood for others. Everyone at the table was lighthearted and excited about going on safari the next morning. There was food and laughter and I don't know why, but sometimes when I see something or feel something and wish I could share it, grief comes like a wave. It hits hard and it overwhelms when it happens. I didn't think anyone would judge me, but I wanted my feelings to be private. Our table was set up in a long room on the second floor of the restaurant, its name I don't remember. Outside, railings surrounded a balcony. I excused myself and stepped out on the balcony alone.

The night was damp from a drizzling rain. I looked down and through the mist I noticed somebody lurking in the bushes. I remember seeing an image in a shadow beneath the balcony and I had a sense that he was watching me. I couldn't make the person out, but I could see he was big and I could see him draw on a cigarette, the flame glowing brighter when he drew on it in the dark. I saw the fire and smoke, not the person.

A few fleeting thoughts went through my mind. *Should I be out here alone? Is it safe? I'm in a foreign country, should I stay with my group?* It felt a little eerie for someone to be lurking in the shadows below. I went from feeling sad to feeling a little fearful.

Matt and Kay came out to check on me.

"We'll stay with you," Kay said. "When you're ready, we'll go back in."

The following day, Frik was again our driver on a long, rugged ride to Kruger National Park for safari--something Gene and I had dreamed of. We stopped alongside a road for a lunch of fruits, cheeses and breads at Danrock Banana Plantation. Fried Plantation Bananas with a scoop of Creme Caramel Pecan ice cream were delivered to our table for an amazing dessert.

After lunch, a host led us through the plantation, telling us about the labor, the need for irrigation to nourish sensitive plants and the cost of shipping to world markets. One thing he said stands out in memory.

"Every month, we need new employees," he told us. "We must replace them."

"Why would you lose employees every month?" The business woman in me asked. My employees had stayed with me for decades, loyal through marriages and births and anniversaries.

"AIDS," our host said. "Every month, they die of AIDS."

Before we boarded, Frik came and sat by me at a picnic table shaded by a low-hanging Jacaranda tree.

"I saw you on the balcony last night," he said. "Are you okay?"

He befriended me. He paid attention to me. And I was so needy.

I started to tell him about my life.

⮌ 3 ⮎

Scottie

More than a thousand people came to Scottie's memorial. There were hundreds who stood in line for two hours to get into the funeral home to honor my son. I was overwhelmed by that, though I know when someone dies young, it is the ultimate loss and people respond in shock and sympathy and probably gratitude because it isn't their son or daughter who died. You have so much influence when you are young and at a pinnacle in life. You touch more people then, as Scottie did in Little League, in business, in the community, in home and family. You are as broad and significant as you'll ever be.

Gene and I were babysitting the grandkids at Scott and Tania's house the day Scottie died. Shannon was splashing around in a bubble bath. She still remembers the moment and so do I.

A few days before, we had stopped by the home Scott and Tania bought when they moved back to Des

Moines after Jack, Scottie's dad (my husband before Gene) died of a massive coronary. His father's fate would become Scottie's fate, too.

Scott had a business in Arizona and when Jack died, he came home to Des Moines to take his dad's place, writing fleet insurance for major truck lines at Donaghy/Kempton.

"I can't do this alone," Jack's partner told Scott. "Come home and help me run the business."

Tania was so very pregnant with Grant then. But they made the decision to move back to their home state. They sold their business, their cars and their house in Arizona and drove from Phoenix to Des Moines in a U-Haul truck. Scott, an only child, was heartbroken about losing his dad, but he loved coming home to Iowa, back to being a Hawkeye fan with all his college buddies.

Their house was full of activity the last day we spent together while Scottie was alive. It seems like it happened in a previous lifetime, although it is always with me, just under the surface. I have often wondered what I am doing here instead of him. It's natural to wonder why.

Tania was packing bags for their trip. Grant was running around in the back yard, wrestling with Lucky, his Golden Lab, the surprise Scottie had given him for Christmas. Shannon doodled with crayons on a little school desk set up in the family room next to the kitchen. The whole house smelled like the Chicken

Piccata Scottie had simmering in garlic butter and capers and lemon juice. Like always, he was doing some chore in the kitchen, chopping celery with his great big hands. He had promised Grant he would teach him to make Chicken Piccata someday.

Their kitchen was the hub of their home. Designed in a large square, windows and a sliding glass patio door looked out over a big yard with lots of space for the kids and the neighborhood. The kitchen looked cluttered, like a family of four lived there. The house fit their lifestyle. Kid's drawings were taped to the refrigerator and canisters, a bag of flour and cooking equipment sat out on the countertops. Tania kept a ceramic piece on the center island. Sometimes, it was a big rooster. That day it was a pink pig. It was darling, I remember. And the kitchen smelled so good.

Scottie was a big guy, a heavy guy, and as he leaned against the kitchen counter, cooking and chopping, he looked heavier than he had been. I walked over beside him and gave him a kiss on the cheek. I looked at him up close, and I didn't like the color in his face or his lips. At six-foot-three and two-hundred-seventy pounds, he was big. He had always been big, but he had blue eyes and a gentle baby face. Normally, he walked with huge strides, as if he had a purpose. A goal. That day, he seemed slow, like to move was a chore. I felt he avoided looking at me.

Head down, he said, "I'm really looking forward to this trip, Mom."

∾

"Are you okay?" I asked. "I don't think your color looks real good."

That was too much mothering.

"Mom! For God's sake," he said. "I know when I'm okay and when I'm not. I've been working hard and Tania and I need this vacation."

"It worries me, Scottie. I know you're not sleeping and sleep apnea can affect all your organs."

He stopped chopping.

"I'm forty-years old, Mom. I can take care of things and I will when I get home. I'll go to that sleep clinic when I get home. Right now, I just need to relax."

Convincing a full-grown man that he had a medical problem and needed to have it taken care of was a hard thing to do, because he wanted to think he was in control and in charge. I knew that, so I backed off, a decision I will regret forever. He was strong-willed, but he wasn't well.

We all hugged when Scott and Tania left for their flight, then Gene and I moved in with the grandkids. When Grant and Shannon woke up the next morning, we had a full day to fill. It was early March, still cold and chilly in Des Moines, so we stayed inside and set up camp in the house. We ordered pizza and started having a good time, making a shambles out of the living room. We moved the sofas and built tents out of the cushions. Shannon dragged blankets from her bed and covered the furniture with them.

Grandpa Gene popped popcorn and we ate it in a tent we'd made. We crawled in and out, laughing and giggling and having a great time. It was a good way to spend a dreary, rainy day. There was a lot of activity in the house. Grant was eleven and was not a quiet boy. Like his dad, he loved to be seen and heard. It was a happy, good time.

By about three o'clock in the afternoon, the kids got bored and I started to think about what we'd have for dinner. Shannon hadn't had her bath yet and she loved her bath time. She gathered her toys and little floaty things and we poured bubble bath that smelled like vanilla into the tub in the upstairs bathroom. Her Barbie dolls always bathed with her. She kept them in a basket beside the tub, Barbies piled high with their arms and legs and hair and little feet sticking out every which way. She yanked off their clothes and plunged them into the bubbles and swam them around with their hair trailing in the water.

She was four-years-old, a darling little thing with soft red curls, plump cheeks and rosy lips. When Scottie would watch a football game in his easy chair, Shannon would curl up and lay like a kitten on his stomach and his shoulder. She was so petite next to him, he'd hold her and you could hardly see her behind Scottie's big hand.

Shannon loved her bath, her girl time. She expected it and she wanted her grandma to be there beside her. So I sat at the edge of the tub, getting splashed.

"Your Barbie dolls are just like your grandma," I told her.

"No, Grandma. They're not."

"I was a little girl when they came into the world," I said. "They got born about the same time I did."

"No, Grandma. They didn't."

"Yes, they did. They wear lots of different outfits, like me. They're even named after me, Barbie."

We laughed and played and splashed and had a ball, Shannon and her Barbies covered in bubbles. Grandpa Gene and Grant were doing boy-things, wrestling around in Grant's bedroom, having an all-out pillow fight. There was a lot of noise and happiness in the house.

Then I heard the phone ring.

~4~

Bringing Scottie Home

Gene answered the phone in the bedroom about three o'clock that Sunday afternoon in March. It was Tania, calling from Cancun while I balanced on the edge of the tub and Shannon splashed in her bubble bath, unaware that the rest of our lives would be lived without Scottie.

I heard Gene say, "No! No! No!"

He walked from the bedroom to the bathroom door and there was a look of horror on his face. His usual, comforting smile was gone. He slumped. I saw pain and agony in his eyes.

He covered the mouthpiece with his hand and said, "Barbie, Scottie died."

He handed the phone to me and I heard Tania crying and sobbing and telling me my son was dead.

"I woke up this morning and something was wrong. I knew it," she sobbed. "I didn't understand why the room felt so quiet. I saw Scott's leg hanging over the edge of the bed outside the blankets and it looked like it was blue."

God, it was awful. I screamed and screamed and screamed and time stopped in that moment with Shannon splashing and Grant playing, their father dead.

"No, Grandma! No, Grandma! He said he'd come home," Grant sobbed, pleading for a different truth. "He said he'd come home."

Then it was chaos. Who we called first, I don't remember. We made contacts and the house that had been filled with fun became overwhelming with constant telephone calls, with people coming to the door, bringing food, cards and flowers, asking what could they do—take care of the kids or the dogs?—with trying to claim Scottie's body and bring him home. With Mexican officials wanting to cremate and Tania refusing to allow it. Scottie had reserved his own cemetery plot at Resthaven next to his dad and that's where he needed to be.

Unraveling the Mexican bureaucracy and bringing Scottie home took days and days and concern for Tania, husbandless, so far away in a foreign country, dealing with grief and loss, frantic with worry about the kids was agonizing. What could we do?

"Come home," I said. "We'll get Scottie home, too." I promised.

* * *

Finally, the agency that had booked the trip to Mexico took charge. They knew how to handle the risks and tragedies of international travel and they arranged to fly Scottie back to Iowa. Then he was home in an open coffin.

"Is this heaven?" Shannon asked when Tania carried her into the funeral home that smelled musky and heavy with the scent of flowers.

I couldn't absorb all that was happening as hundreds of people surrounded us to offer comfort and tributes. I remember that it seemed like a gathering, more like a receiving line than a wake. I felt the necessity to try to make people comfortable as if they were guests, not mourners, to talk to them and greet them and thank them for their condolences, to stay strong and say I was doing okay because that's what they wanted to know. I functioned in a state of shock, in a reprieve the body and mind allowed before the grip of grief and anger, regret and sorrow, blame and uncertainty, hurt and fear took hold.

There is no explanation for what or why one thing is remembered and others are forgotten in mourning, but I hold a picture of my brother Jerry in my mind. I felt shaky and weak at one point during the memorial, and he took my arm and led me into another room.

"You need to come with me," he said. "You don't look good. You've been standing up all night. Come and sit down with me."

He is my younger brother, my baby brother, good-looking and articulate. The most outspoken member of the family, he comes off as strong and self-assured, but he's a two-sided coin and he becomes sensitive and compassionate when he's needed.

I remember him putting his arm around me and ushering me through an arched doorway, as if we were moving from one room to another and one life to another, nothing seeming real.

"Take a couple of deep breaths," he said.

He sat beside me at a little table and brought me something to drink, a juice of some kind. Something cold.

He wore a dark mustache. I remember the moment, like it's a little snapshot.

Gene gave me sedatives that night and I tried to sleep before the funeral the following morning. There were a lot of people still in the house, friends and neighbors, family, brothers and sisters.

Was that when Scottie died? Or Gene? I don't remember and that distresses me. Whose funeral am I remembering?

The feeling of uncertainty that never goes away has stayed with me all these years and I think it always will. When I drive into the cemetery, I feel anxious when I have to make a choice. Who I will go see first? If I choose Scottie before Gene, does it mean I cared more for one than the other? I don't want to make choices. I want to love them both.

～5～

Grant

The images in my mind are still of those children, my grandchildren who should have their daddy. I felt that Grant was the lost person in this.

"Grandma, I can't stay in this house," he said after his dad's funeral while relatives and friends milled about. Adults had come to console Tania and me before and after the funeral, but how do children cope?

Grant would eventually go to a grief counselor, a psychologist, and after a long time, he'd learn to open up, little bits at a time. Before then, what he did to protect himself was grab his baseball and his glove and his Little League jacket with the Cardinal emblem on the front and his name on the back. He zipped up his jacket and zipped up his feelings.

He went out in the yard, all alone except for his dog, Lucky. I never saw him cry over his dad again.

∾ 6 ∾

Gene

*H*ow does life look at its happiest? Snapshots tell the story. But my boxes of photographs and keepsakes stayed in storage for years, in a way buried there because I couldn't make myself sort through reminders of the before and after. The fullness of life before and the emptiness after.

The thing about death is that it is incomprehensible. They are there one minute and then they're not.

You can't believe it and you can't understand.

Ask anyone who has lost someone and they will say that, no matter how prepared we think we are, when life becomes death, we cannot comprehend.

How can this be? He looked at me. He spoke to me. He loved me and I loved him.

In that darkest year, the shock numbed. Little by little, my mind allowed me to reach back in time and let memory build a bridge between the world I had known and the world that was suddenly unrecognizable without Scottie and Gene. Piece by piece, happy,

∾

bright and even funny memories started to come forward out of the sadness. And it is the memories, not the photos, that are real—like the night of Gene's surprise birthday party in a December blizzard that, even by Central Iowa standards, was huge.

Invitations had been mailed to one-hundred and fifty friends and relatives, letting them in on the surprise celebration—*60 Years in the Fast Lane*. The people at Ostrem Imports picked up the theme and offered to hold the party in their service garage, not the showroom. The design on the invitation showed a sports car with a man and a woman speeding along, the wind blowing their hair. The message read:

Black Tie and Tennis Shoes. Deodorant Optional.

LaValle, the best caterer in the city who was known by one name, planned the menu—pyramids of fresh fruits, imported cheeses and nuts. Coconut Shrimp and Smoked Salmon and Trout. A fountain of champagne and chocolate.

He laid a flat board over huge hydraulic lifts that raise cars up for servicing. He draped the lifts in white linens and converted them to serving tables with platters of his specialty hors d' oeuvres presented like works of beautiful and funky art. New Goodyear radials, also covered in white linens, became serving pieces with pastries and fresh breads arranged in the hollow of the tires, like flowers in a basket.

The decorator was coming in from Kansas City, a three-hour drive in a van packed with props and decorations. Massive floral arrangements were to stand on columns and pedestals and huge red ribbons would be wrapped around each new car—Mercedes, Jags, and BMW's. A disc jockey had been hired, the bay area at the car dealer's had been scrubbed clean and a dance floor was installed under a mirrored ball that hung overhead like it was prom night in a gymnasium. And a remote-controlled race track was set up in back.

It was a grand plan. Keeping it under the radar and keeping it from Gene was not easy. Being an accountant and an actuary, Gene kept track of details and it was hard to withhold information from him, though the party was scheduled ahead of his birthday so he wouldn't be suspicious.

The day arrived with everything in place. Until it started to snow.

Maybe it won't be too bad, I thought. Maybe it will quit.

But it didn't quit. Hour by hour, the storm got worse until there was a total white out with snowdrifts four feet deep and highways in and out of town became sheets of ice. The decorator from Kansas City hadn't shown up and hadn't called.

Where is he, I wondered. Is he okay and will he make it? How is this party going to come off? The blizzard is getting worse. I'm not sure anyone will make it. What's going to happen when Gene and I get there? Will anybody be there?

By four o'clock, the receptionist at Ostrem Imports took a call from Frank, the decorator. He had hit sleet at the Iowa border and said it was like a curtain of ice had come down. He said he'd never been so scared in his life. His van loaded with decorations skidded off the road and was stuck in a deep ravine. Someone—I don't remember who, maybe it was Scottie—recruited a tow truck and drove out to rescue the decorator and haul the van out of a bottomless ravine. He made it into town an hour before the party and Frank threw decorations together like it was a magic show. With columns and ribbons and statues and bows, he turned a garage into a party room for whoever would show up in the midst of a blizzard.

"Why do we have to wear a tuxedo to go to dinner at Sunnie and Roger's?" Gene asked before getting dressed.

"I don't know. It's a formal dinner," I said. "It's important to them."

He had laid his tuxedo out on the bed in our all-white bedroom. I remember it looked artsy with Gene's tux spread across the bed on a white duvet, like it was a focal point in a black and white photo. An acrylic chair that looked transparent sat in the corner of the bedroom and beneath it, I remember seeing Gene's black dress shoes with stockings stuffed into one shoe. He didn't know he was supposed to wear tennis shoes.

How nice the tux will look on him, I thought.

I leaned into the mirror, putting on make up and false eyelashes in the bathroom vanity. The phone in the bedroom rang and I heard Gene talking, agreeing to something. The call was part of the scheme to get Gene to the party.

"That was Roger," he said. "Now we have to go by Ostrem's and pick up Roger's friends from Chicago. They had to take their car in for something and they need a ride.

"I don't know why we're doing this at all. With the weather so bad," he said.

"I think we have to."

I had hidden two pairs of tennis shoes, his and mine, in a bag by the door. I grabbed the bag and draped my coat over my arm to conceal the bag on our way to the car.

"Here, give me your coat. You'd better put it on," Gene offered. He looked so handsome.

"No, I'll carry it. I don't want to put it over my out-fit," I said.

Snow was still falling non-stop and amazingly, we didn't have much trouble plowing through on Grand Avenue. Grand is the major route to the capital build-ing and the governor's mansion, so it's kept fairly open, no matter the weather. I couldn't imagine how anyone else would get there, or who would want to on a night like that.

We drove up to the back of Ostrem's and when the big garage door opened, about one hundred people who had made it through the blizzard yelled surprise. It was a surprise to me, too, though I should have known, a blizzard doesn't stop people who live in Iowa.

Scottie was at the front of the crowd, wearing a tuxedo and cummerbund and I think he was kind of thrilled because he liked to dress well and he hadn't worn formal wear since he and Tania were married. Tania was there, decked out in high-heeled shoes and shooting video with her new camera.

Roger and Sunnie made it through snowdrifts and slick roads—they'd been in on it from the beginning—and Sunnie looked fabulous in a black formal dress with a sequined skirt.

"Look!" she said. She lifted her skirt and under her formal gown, she wore red tennis shoes with sequins glued on. Roger wore his old high-tops, like he was still a jock in high school.

My sister Marty was there from Kansas City. Gene's brother Larry had flown in from Houston ahead of the storm. And Gene's friends and business associates and their wives, all in tuxedos, gowns and tennis shoes crowded around. We danced and ate and talked and played and, thanks to Frank and his last-minute rescue from a ditch by the side of road, the place looked marvelous. The big attraction was the race track in the back room. Grown men, CEOs who ran huge companies sat around in their tuxedos with remote controls in their hands, steering little cars around a toy race track.

The theme of the party was accurate. Gene and I had been living in the fast lane with international travel in a world of friends and family and exciting experiences and so much happiness that began the day we met.

My life has been too perfect, I'd sometimes think. *What's going to happen? Everyone deals with problems— why am I sailing along having this great life when there are people who suffer? When will the other shoe drop?*

Our life together started at the mailbox in the Warren House on University Avenue where Gene and I had apartments while we were both in a transition. We had each been married before and were out on our own in apartment-house living. I had noticed him at different functions in Des Moines and I made it a point to find out who he was. He was good-looking and bright and seemed to be kind. He dressed well and was known for his wonderful, trademark smile that was friendly and comforting. Several days in a row, we turned up in the lobby, checking our mail at the same time. I decided to take a risk.

"I think you should take me out to dinner," I said.

He looked at me, a little surprised, and said, "You think so?"

"Yeah, because I think we'd have a good time," I said.

"We could try that sometime," he said.

More than a week went by.

Then I saw him again at the mailbox and he asked if I'd like to go out to dinner—but it didn't turn out to be dinner.

~

He drove me out to Walnut Woods, a park on the Raccoon River and I couldn't believe what I saw. He pulled a blanket out of the trunk of the car and spread it on the ground under a grove of trees. He'd brought a picnic basket and he had packed a lunch with apples, cheese, bread, carrot cake and wine and real wine glasses, not plastic. He'd put it all together himself which was charming to me.

He sliced the apples with the Swiss Army knife he had carried with him for all his days.

Who has the knife now? I don't remember.

Gene poured wine into the stemmed glasses and I sipped a bit of it because I didn't want to tell him that I don't drink and, like my dad, never have. I felt like a princess who was taken on a picnic and I had thought we'd just go get a hamburger. But from then on, Gene brought a classy, European kind of style to my life until he got sick.

* * *

It wasn't long before we decided to get married and since we had each been married before, we didn't want an outlandish wedding. Gene thought it would be romantic—it was so sweet—if we'd get married at The Little Brown Church in the Vale. It had been made famous by a song, *Come, come, come, come to the church in the wildwood...Come to the church in the vale.* It was secluded and quaint.

On a gorgeous October day, we stood as a group on the steps of the church in a wooded area with the trees already turning for fall. The wedding party was immediate family. Gene's daughters, Shelley and Tracy were with us. Gene's mother and her sister were there, all dressed up in gloves and hats. Mom was no longer alive and Dad couldn't make it because he was in the hospital. Everyone in the wedding party was there, except Scottie, the best man.

It's getting late. Where's Scottie?

I was feeling a little nervous, wondering where Scottie could be. Then we heard music blaring from somewhere in the distance, and along came Scott and his forever friend, Scottie Moore, driving toward the church in a beat-up van. We heard the music before we saw them bopping and singing with the stereo booming full blast, and then we saw the van and heard the music as they sailed right on by.

What's he doing? Where's he going? Scottie!

We couldn't believe it. The best man drove on down the road. Then the sound of music came closer again and the van was on its way back. They pulled up in front of the church and Scottie unfolded his six-foot-three frame and he was so cute and skinny and tall then. Before the wedding, he had gone to Gene's hairstylist who talked him into getting a perm so he stood on the altar like a pole in his 1970s plaid suit and his giant head of frizzy and blonde Afro hair.

The wedding lasted only about fifteen minutes and before it began, the church people locked the doors so the next wedding party wouldn't come in halfway through our ceremony. We were ready to say our vows and I noticed motion (or a commotion) outside, beyond a stained glass window. It looked like someone was jumping up and down and someone was. Ann and Don Beeson, friends of ours, arrived late and were locked out and were outside, bobbing up and down and trying to peek through the window to see us get married.

Built by homesteaders, the little church has stood on limestone for more than one hundred years. It's tiny and picturesque with hardly ten rows of church pews on the inside. Three houses and the church are all there is in the woods along Iowa's Cedar River, but the church ladies have a thriving business, catering receptions for a calendar filled with wedding ceremonies each year. They hosted ours and after the wedding, we went downstairs to the church basement and (I'm not kidding), the church ladies served lime Jello with pears in it and egg salad sandwiches on white bread with the crusts trimmed off and Cheez Whiz on crackers as hors d' oeuvres.

It was like Tony and Tina's wedding. And we wouldn't have traded it for anything.

"You love Gene because he's handsome and rich," someone once said. It was Rosie Schneider—a woman who used to be in my life.

"If Gene lost every cent he has, I would love him," I said. "I've never known a man like him."

With Gene and his daughters and Scottie and Tania and our grandkids, we were a portrait of a contented blended family. I knew it. Yet I never took happiness for granted and it wasn't that I hadn't paid a price. Scottie was just a baby when his dad, Jack, was diagnosed and went through months of treatment for cancer. The medical bills and debt piled up and we struggled to pay the mortgage on the little house we had and though Jack recovered from cancer, he still died young. I hadn't just danced along before I met Gene and I had a sense that I wouldn't get out of this world unscathed. There was a stronger feeling that things felt perfect, like happily-ever-after in a fairytale. And for twenty-five years with Gene at my side, the fairy tale was real.

* * *

I know now that when I met Frik in South Africa, he was handsome and charming like my son and my husband had been and I wanted him to fill the emptiness. I needed to believe.

If I can bring Frik home to America, I can have that perfect life again, I thought. *Gene won't be there and Scottie won't be there. Frik can step in and I can make a whole life again.*

In some way, God had a hand in helping me believe that someone would stay with me and love me and not leave me alone. I held that hope, trying to cope until I was strong enough to leave South Africa and go home to the house on Bay Hill where ambulance attendants had covered Gene with a white sheet and carried him out through the front door on a gurney. When everyone was gone and families and friends had returned to their lives, as they should, after Scottie's funeral, Gene's dry cough was like an echo in the quiet of the house. The cough had been misdiagnosed a few months earlier. This time, three weeks after Scottie was buried, x-rays revealed Gene's lung cancer. Stage Four.

Emergency lights on the ambulance flashed red in the drive outside the house the night he died. Kindly, the attendants waited a few minutes after they arrived until we—Gene's daughters, my sister and I—could begin to realize he was gone.

~7~

Friends and White Roses

The house where we lived and the house where Gene died was eventually sold. He had had his favorite spot, a butter-colored leather chair near a bay window overlooking a lake. An estate sale emptied that nook and stripped the rooms and the walls so the days and nights of a new family could begin on Bay Hill Drive.

I would in time go to South Africa. But in the months before, I was alone in the house with a For Sale sign in front. I tried to fill empty hours by writing thank you notes and sifting through boxes and baskets overflowing with cards and condolences.

Every card and kindness mattered. One gift I remember even today is a small, modest bouquet sent by Art Filean with a personal note tucked inside. It is as clear in my memory as if he'd sent it this morning— a simple bouquet of beautiful white roses in a dainty round vase, also white, each rose small and perfect as a baby. Art was Secretary of a corporate board and I had served alongside him. He called for months and months after Scottie and Gene died. I'd talk to him and cry and there was Art, a kind man who didn't know what to do or say. So he just listened. I don't see him much now that he's retired, but he looked after me for so long. Other friends, like Gloria, Roger, Sunnie and so many more looked after me, too.

Anywhere in the world Roger and Sunnie went for years after Gene and Scottie died, they'd call on holidays. They still do.

Both Roger and Gene became heads of companies and both had started out as hard-working Iowa farm boys. Roger shouldered the responsibility of running the farm after his father died suddenly when Roger was only thirteen. He took over as the man in the family, a driven man who is relentless when it comes to making hard decisions and doing what he has to do. He can be intimidating, but Gene and I learned to know his softer side. He came to the house a few hours before Gene died and he tried to put on a brave front, but he was shaken. Nobody thought Gene could be gone—he was the strongest, the healthiest, the most active. He didn't drink. He didn't smoke. He ran five miles four times a week. When other men saw how cancer so quickly ravaged him, I think it touched their own sense of mortality.

Roger was there in Gene's final hours and he was there for me when I tried to begin again. He came over to do guy things when the house on Bay Hill sold and

I moved into a downtown loft. He and Sunnie had been to dinner with Joyce and Rick Chapman and they all stopped by to help me get settled. They brought cheese and wine and grapes and crackers and Roger came through the door carrying a handful of tools like he was a man with a mission.

"What do you wanna have done? What do we need to do? You gotta get these boxes out of here. They're empty," he said, answering his own questions.

He broke down the boxes, smashed them with his foot, folded them and stacked them in a pile by the door, clearing out the corner. Sunnie and Joyce unpacked a tray and set cheese and grapes out on the counter.

"What else do you want?" Roger asked.

"I was going to try to hang that big mirror."

"Where do you want it?"

"I'd like to hang it over that table in the foyer," I said. "It's too heavy for me to handle."

"I can do this," he let me know.

The loft feels homey now, but it was a major change from the house on Bay Hill. It's a small, modern space in a converted nineteenth-century warehouse on Market Street in downtown Des Moines. Walls are exposed brick, industrial pipes hang overhead and outside my door, corridors are wide enough to ride a bicycle down the hall. Gene and I had looked at the lofts when they were under development and we loved the windows, so huge that when I walk in, the whole outdoors is waiting in the living room. It overlooks the Des Moines River and a bridge that leads to Gray's Lake where there's a memorial plaque for Scottie and Gene along a walkway. I held special pieces out of the estate sale and lined the loft entrance with art, some of Gene's favorite pieces, one from Czechoslovakia, his ancestral country.

That night, Sunnie and Joyce and I unpacked dishes and stacked them in kitchen cupboards, trying to make the loft a home. Then Roger came into the kitchen, both arms swinging, tools in hand and totally in charge.

"What else do you need?"

"Well, I have these knobs," I said. "I wanted them to go on the dresser drawers in the bedroom."

"I can do that!"

Off he went, clutching his tools and a plastic bag with thirty-two knobs of stainless steel. Joyce and Sunnie and I were in the kitchen, just being together, talking and putting things away when Roger came back, mission accomplished—not only getting me settled, but making sure I didn't feel abandoned.

"Got the knobs on your dresser," he said. "But I gotta tell you something. It looks to me like you need new underwear."

He laughed, like he thought he was really funny, like he'd been snooping in a woman's underwear drawer. Roger doesn't want to seem too soft and cuddly, so he gives people, especially me, a hard time. That's how I know he loves me.

⌐

In the legion of friends, there's another one who will stand by me forever. You'd think Gloria and I would be a mismatch because we're so different. She lived most of her life in Omaha and that alone says a lot. She is small and Italian. I'm tall and Scotch Irish. She wears her hair gray, shaped into a blunt cut. Mine is short and blonde, casual and spikey. She raised two daughters and a son and I raised Scottie. She's educated and bright and she quit teaching to stay home and be a housewife and a mother. I started out as an x-ray technician, then stepped out of the mold to build businesses. Gloria was the perfect picture of The Corporate wife, a reflection of the conservative, family-owned company. I never fit in as The Corporate wife. I didn't fit the mold.

The founder ran the company well into his eighties and his rigid philosophy held: Never look too rich or successful. Never outshine your customer. Never wear facial hair. Drive Chevrolets and Fords because that's Middle America. Wives stay home and take care of the family. Wives don't work.

His daughter wasn't warm or friendly to anyone, but her daddy owned the company and the wives followed her lead. She was very much in control and very much not my fan. It was a political situation and I realize now that often, the one who is different is excluded from the group.

I was the "second wife" and a working woman which were both taboo, according to The Corporation traditions. I had owned and managed my own business since before Jack died. Birth control had given women new freedom and activists like Gloria Steinam came out of the feminist movement and led women into the ranks of commerce. The 1970s became a different world, but the male culture was dominant and, in Des Moines, few women were in business. A bank loan required three Cs: Credit. Character. Collateral. Women might have had character, but most had no credit. Neither did I.

The job I landed as a headhunter in an employment agency pushed me toward the freedoms of the feminist movement. Women who were in their fifties would come into the agency after going through a divorce and it was so sad. They were at a low point in their lives when they needed to use their own resources and make a living on their own, though they hadn't been on their own before.

How can I help find a job for them? They have no work experience and they're so desperate, I remember thinking. *I won't let myself end up in a place where I'm dependent on someone else. I want to stand on my own and take control of my own destiny and not end up in an employment agency someday, trying to find a job that will barely pay the rent.*

That's when I signed a loan. A former partner of Jack's took a chance, backed me on a bank loan and I opened my first Merle Norman Cosmetic Studio in Merle Hay Mall in Des Moines. The loan covered more than fifty-thousand dollars for store fixtures, flooring and inventory. I wrote the checks and took them to the mailbox and stood there, too terrified to drop the envelopes into the slot. I remember thinking, *If I mail these checks, I'll be in debt. If they cash them, I'll be in debt. If I don't mail them, I can go back to the bank and return the money and say I'm not going to do this and they'll be happy.*

I pulled the handle on the mailbox, sent the checks and set my life in a new direction. I went back into the mall and looked over the space I'd rented and thought, *Wow! I have a lot to do.*

I had stepped out of the circle into unknown territory and plenty of critics predicted that I would fail. Eventually, though, I bought out my partner and owned and managed three of the country's top-ranking Gold Medal Merle Norman studios, plus a manufacturing plant and I accepted an appointment to the board of an international investment and securities company, the largest 401-K provider in America.

But the critics were right. In the beginning, I failed.

I wasn't married and I had a mortgage, rent to pay on the store and a bank loan. Building the business took every bit of time, energy and money I could find and there wasn't enough income to draw a salary. The store didn't make enough to meet expenses in the beginning and I felt like a failure. So I called my old boss at the employment agency and asked if I could come back. That meant working a day job, working at the store nights and weekends and pouring the agency paycheck into the business for two years. By the time

Gene and I met, I had made my way. My financials were strong and he discovered I could play golf, too. I can hit a ball as far as most men, one-hundred eighty yards down the fairway, like my dad taught me.

I told Dad before he died that Gene fell in love with me for two reasons: I have a good golf swing and a good bottom line.

* * *

Gene and I were alike in so many ways and so different in others. We were raised in small farming communities in Iowa. His was an acreage in a county seat town of seven-thousand people, not far from Iowa City. His was a typical all-American community of the 1950s with a fountain and summer band concerts in the courthouse square. He served in the Army, stationed in Germany and he was proud to get his education with the G.I. Bill.

I grew up in Emmetsburg, a county seat of five-thousand people, also with summer night band concerts on the courthouse square. But I grew up on Five Island Lake, a hub for boating and swimming in summer and skating and ice fishing in winter. And unlike Gene, I could escape to another world. We lived only miles away from the Roof Garden, an open-air ballroom on Lake Okoboji, and we danced to The Glenn Miller Orchestra and Duke Ellington all summer long. Big swing bands were later replaced by teenage heartthrobs made famous on American Bandstand and we rock and rolled to The Big Bopper and Fabian (who wheeled through Emmetsburg in a white Cadillac convertible with his hair slicked back like he was Elvis).

Everyone in my family was fun-loving, so opinionated and strong that our supper table conversation was a main event. Gene came from an entirely different kind of family, one that was so reserved, you could hear their knives and forks click the plates when they ate. He was quiet and conforming; I don't hold back.

"You can't wear that," he said one winter night when I put on a full-length mink for The Corporate party.

"Why not?" It was Christmas and it was cold.

"It doesn't look right, Barb," he said. "Nobody wears those kinds of things there. You would just stand out."

"Yeah! That's the point," I said.

"I don't know what the founder would think."

"It's gorgeous. And it's warm. And it's practical in Iowa," I said. "I could catch pneumonia if I don't wear it."

I did stand out. And for that, I stood alone, except for Gloria who stood beside me. It was because of our husbands who worked together at The Corporation that we met. And it was The Corporation that could have pulled us apart.

In those years, Gloria and I would lunch and talk on our own, then she'd follow along with the other wives because of her husband and his job and what her role

∾

was expected to be. But there was always something special about Gloria.

"You're a lot more outgoing than I am," she'd say. "I probably hold back my feelings. Maybe I shouldn't."

What she might have wanted to do was teach, she told me. What she decided to do was to be The Corporate wife; in some ways, she still is. She and Larry have moved to Arizona, not far from the home Gene and I bought in the high desert before he died. Gloria doesn't venture out too far without Larry, but she'll drive the twenty-five mile stretch to my place since she knows Scottsdale Road is a straight shot.

"I don't drive anywhere unless I can make right turns," she reminds me.

And I remind her, "Gloria, if you continue to make only right turns, you'll be going around in circles."

When we're both in Arizona, I pick her up and I drive and I turn left and I go off the beaten path—and Gloria goes with me. We love to lunch on the open-air tier at the Nieman Marcus store in Fashion Square Mall, especially when its springtime in the desert. A breeze blows across our table and hummingbirds hover in the bougainvillea vines that climb an outdoor trellis. We can smell the perfume. We order the spinach salad topped with strawberries and pears and goat cheese and crunchy pecans, served like a work of art on china plates with sterling flatware.

"Gloria, where's your diamond pendant?" I asked one day at lunch. "You're not wearing it."

She wears expensive jewelry, diamond stud earrings and an impressive diamond pendant on a chain, like so many women do.

"You told me it looked like a headlight," she said.

I had.

I didn't know she'd take it so seriously but, yes, I'd told her those diamond pendants show no creativity. "It looks like your security, Gloria," I said. "It says, 'look at the diamond on my neck—aren't I rich? It looks like a big headlight hanging there announcing that you have resources."

"You just come right out with it, Barb. I like that you're honest," she said. "There are very few honest people. I try to be. But a lot of people don't like honesty because they'd rather have things sugared."

She held out her hand. And there was the big diamond on her finger.

"I had the headlight made into a ring," she said.

When I came home from South Africa—after Frik and I had been hijacked and shot and it had been in the news—Gloria said she thinks I like to shock people.

"No, Gloria. I don't like to shock people," I said. "But I don't say no to life. If you hide from life, if you don't take risks, you can end up with regrets. I regret that Scottie and Gene died. But that's not really regret. That's sadness."

Through the years, strong friendships helped take me through dark hours. And by now, after thirty years, Gloria and I know what to expect from one another and what to say. Our conversations are genuine. Our differences have become harmonious. She is a source of strength, this woman I never thought would say boo or shit, if her mouth was full of it.

I look back every day—I can't help it—and I long for what was, but I'm grateful for all my friends. With Gloria, I'm true to my instincts. And Gloria is true to hers. I bring energy and enthusiasm and action into her life. She brings support and history and loyalty to mine. She's a little like the white roses sent by Art Filean, a tasteful and unpretentious woman, so special in that way.

～8～

First Run at First Light

When someone hears that I lost my son and my husband within six months of one another and then I was shot in South Africa, they say, "You were shot in South Africa?" That's the story most people want to know. That's the story that carried me, step by step, to a place of courage so I could take the road home and face what had to be faced. But I had no idea what I would face in South Africa.

After Danroc Plantation, we boarded again and followed the scenic road along the slopes of the six-hundred mile Drakensberg Mountain range, the route to Kruger National Park and safari. We stopped to rest at botanical centers called Blooms and Beasts where, as our brochures promised, South African fauna, flora and history dazzled us.

The first night out, we lodged at a roadside village with a modern hotel and casino. After dark, there was a party atmosphere in the camp and I didn't feel up to the revelry so I stayed in my room to retreat. We met

～

the next morning and a woman in the group said, "Frik was worried about you. He waited outside your door last night and you didn't come out. He thought we should go check on you."

We were walking through a botanical center at the time. Frik was in the group and he joined me on the garden path.

"How are you doing?" He asked. That accent!

I said I was fine and I thought, *That's interesting. That he cares about me. That he seems to seek me out. Does he feel sorry for me?*

He stayed near my side on the garden tour, attentively, until we boarded and left again, en route to Kruger Park with a stop on a mountain top that evening. Our hosts organized a cookout and when Frik let me out of the tour bus, he said, "Go ahead. I'll join you."

I liked spending time with him. It seemed special that this handsome, kind man paid attention to me when I felt so alone. Many times, Frik didn't go where the group went, like into the market places, because he stayed behind with the vehicle. I'd go and talk to him and spend time with him while others in my group shopped for souvenirs.

I didn't think about status, that Frik was a working man and I was a widow with indulgences and freedoms and the means to travel and pay my own way. His lifestyle was modest, not poor, and in comparison, mine was privileged. But he had what I no longer had, parents and children. He had attachments and I had none. He drove a bus and I was floating around the world as a traveler. Yet we had started to build a connection and there was no reason to feel discomfort or to think of our differences.

What mattered was that Frik was bright and articulate. I felt he could teach me about his culture and his country. Knowing him, I began to realize that in South Africa, people do what they need to do to make a living. The country seemed to be entrepreneurial in the absence of huge corporations, like the big American conglomerates. Our differences, Frik's and mine, may have been economic, but I didn't feel that separation at the time.

We pushed on and when we arrived at Kruger Park, a gate opened and closed behind us as we pulled into the lodge complex. The people there, not the animals, are fenced in, our guide explained. The park is open. Animals are respected and allowed to prowl and hunt at night. They'd come into the lodge area if it weren't fenced in, he said.

When I stepped out of the bus, I noticed a small black woman who was sweeping the street and the walkway. All around the complex, women carried baskets and pots on their heads as they crossed the grounds under a calming, blue sky. She, this little black woman, looked at us and gave us a gracious smile, like a genuine kindness and contentment we Americans seem to have lost.

The lodge was massive and rugged, like cabins I had seen in Canada on fishing expeditions with my dad when we were kids. It was a huge wooden structure with a porch all around and inside, a stone fireplace. Tables in the dining area were covered in white linen for a touch of class in contrast to the ruggedness. Chandeliers hung from high ceilings and the light seemed to glow, not in a cold white light but in a warm amber. The keeper of the lodge welcomed us in English and to show the beauty of his native language, he also greeted us in Afrikaan. Hosts were extremely polite and they spoke English fluently, but their special brand of gentility came from the European influence and the culture of South Africa, I thought. Nobody seemed hurried or pushy. They never said, huh? Or what? They said, I beg your pardon, ma'am. It was nice.

There in what I had expected to be the wild, the beauty of the people and the luxury and accommodations of the lodge seemed without end. Shaggy brush and trees were visible outdoors, but indoors the lodge was comfortable and warm and welcoming.

We slept that night in thatch-roofed huts set in a circle across from the main lodge. I noticed a strong, earthy scent from the thatched roof when I entered the room. The smell reminded me of the hayloft where my brothers and sister and I played on our grandpa's farm when we were young. The straw on the hut had been there a long time and it was mixed with clay, but it smelled like hay and it took me home to memories of the farm in Iowa.

The bed's rough, wooden frame looked like it was made of sticks. The mattress and pillow were thin and there was no bedspread, but bedding was clean and dazzling white in contrast to the room's darkness. African masks handmade by the Zulu were nailed to the walls as colorful and primitive decorations. Though spartan, the room was serviceable with a shower, night stand, chest of drawers and a foot locker for my luggage.

I had chosen to be alone in single quarters. Because of where I was in my heart and mind, I didn't want to share a room with anyone, which seems like the opposite of what I should have felt. More than once, I regretted my choice because I felt isolated and fearful since I could hear animals rustling outside the windows, making sounds that were unfamiliar, not loud noises, but moans and howls and whines like big distant cats. Uncertainty ran through my mind.

Should I have chosen differently? Should I have stayed with someone? Am I truly alone? Am I safe by myself?

I unpacked and walked to the lodge to join the others for dinner and an orientation about safari. It was a fun, lively evening and in the magnificence of the experience, I wished I could share it with Scottie and Gene. I looked at people laughing and talking around the fireplace and I wondered, *do you know how lucky you are?*

We broke up early, sometime before ten o'clock because we'd need to be awake and ready to go by four-thirty the next morning to take a first run at safari.

"Okay, we've gotta get to bed," I said. "I didn't know I'd need an alarm clock on safari."

A guide walked me to my hut and I slid into bed, alone in the pitch black night with no light out in the bush and no artificial light in the yard. I laid awake in the bed, flat as the mattress, with arms crossed over my chest, waiting for night to pass, not sleeping but dozing with one eye open, like a cowboy in a western movie, alert to any sound of rustling in the bush.

I don't know why I felt unsafe, but it was a new country and a new feeling. I'd come out of a luxurious environment and before I lost Scottie and Gene, I had always felt safe and secure and never alone. I was still awake when a guide from Rhino Tripping Safari, our tour operator, came to the hut. He knew I didn't have an alarm clock so he rapped on my door, hours before dawn, called first light in South Africa. Coming from the city, I hadn't realized we'd see few animals during the day. Outings were very early morning and after dinner at night. That was the way of safari.

~ 9 ~

Safari

T he weather was cool. The sky was dark. Dressed in jackets against the chill, we settled into a big vehicle, like a Humvee with an open top. Besides the drivers, two gunmen were on board, one in the front and one in the back. If I close my eyes, I can picture us moving through a morning that is pitch black except for spotlights mounted on the truck, scanning the lower part of the bush. It was a rough ride and we drove into deep ravines, down by waterways.

We watched. We stopped. We spotted flashing eyes.

There stood a hyena with eyes fiery in the dark, like when a flash bulb goes off and eyes glow red on film. His body was sleek and gray and muscled. He stood completely still and stared at the truck, protecting his pack. Behind him, other hyenas moved in the bush, but this one held his ground in confrontation, ready to charge if we came any closer. It was our first sighting.

The guides had told us that if we saw the Big Five—lion, leopard, elephant, water buffalo, rhinoceros—

~

we'd have a successful safari. And we did before we left Kruger. The lion was the most majestic, but the elephants were beautiful, too.

After daybreak, we followed an elephant herd that let us come so close I could see the bristles on their hide and I felt the clumps of dirt they tossed into the air pelting my head and back. It was amazing to watch the way they functioned in their habitat, the way they rubbed one another and clustered in families and looked after others in the herd. They fanned their big ears, moving them forward, then back again, a motion that made me think they were picking up sounds, like our voices. They watched and listened, assessing danger, sensing that humans were near. They sniffed the air and touched their trunks together and made low moans to communicate. They moved with a slow lumber and incredible grace despite their size. They seemed to be so nurturing, so loving to their little calves. Up close, I saw that their big eyes were also warm and beautiful. They were big, but elegant, especially when I realized we were so close to the descendants of giant, pre-historic creatures that had roamed the earth and have a softness and magnificence about them. They were gentle giants, like my son had been. Big, strong, sensitive and mild.

The experience was humbling, one of many lessons learned in the wild. Other experiences were stark and gruesome and there was a law of the jungle I'll never forget. We watched an act of violence in horror as a male zebra stomped a baby zebra to death and the anguished mother whinnied and screamed, helplessly watching her baby die.

"My, God! That's terrible," I said. "Can't somebody do something about that?"

"She's his mate, but that's not his child," Frik said. "She made it with another. Animals will do that. They know by scent."

The mother had delivered the baby zebra, but her mate was not the father so he stomped and crushed the baby until it died.

"That's how nature works. If you have a mate, you don't have somebody else's baby," Frik said.

It was sad to share the experience and witness such extreme violence in a gorgeous animal that is usually placid. It was heartbreaking and horrifying and fascinating and yet, we watched. I didn't turn away.

On safari, Frik was a companion and a passenger, like me. He kept a seat beside me and I enjoyed his company as we drove deeper and deeper into Kruger. Safari continued for two nights and days and we moved from campsite to campsite along the trails with each stop its own experience. At night, Frik made sure I got safely to my room.

Campsites on safari were authentic, not luxurious. But Matt Rosen, our organizer, scheduled one lavish night in a modern resort and built the cost into the price of the trip. I think it was called Thornybush Shumbalala Game Lodge and it was as magnificent as any hotel Gene and I had stayed in anywhere in the world, from Aspen to London, Rome or Prague. I could picture the lodge laid out as a spread in Architectural Digest with its walkways all around and glass all across the back that overlooked shaggy foliage of the bush with a river running through. Armed guards stationed outside the resort protected us from animals that roamed the river at night. All of Kruger Park was fenced, but the lodge was not and we were assigned companions when we crossed the grounds. Most of the building was open and breathtakingly beautiful with gauzy curtains instead of walls. My bed was draped in white netting to keep flying insects away. The shower was outdoors.

This is thrilling, I thought. *I feel like a queen.*

Then I opened the closet and four slimy lizards ran out. In that wonderful room! I started to attack them with the tip of an umbrella and screamed for someone to help.

Frik came running in.

"Settle down," he said. "They're more afraid of you than you are of them."

"They almost gave me a heart attack," I said. "I don't want lizards crawling over me while I'm in bed."

"They're everywhere in South Africa and they'll run from you," he said.

"What if they get in my suitcase? What if everything I take out has a lizard in it?"

"They don't want to be confined in your suitcase," he said.

I was petrified. There were huge wild animals in the bush, yet the little lizards gave me the creeps. Frik promised he'd come back to check on me and escort me to the main lodge for evening activities. I laid my clothes out for dinner with the group and a few hours of socializing around the lit fireplace in the main lodge. I tied a bandana around my head, probably thinking it was a chic look. At one point in the evening, I felt a heavy sadness in the relaxed environment and I was quiet, lost in thought. So many times, and that was one them, I felt that my life had ended. I believed I'd never have another reason to truly celebrate. I'd never have another dinner party or a son who'd come over for a backyard barbecue and say, "Mom, can I have a beer?" Dawn Taylor noticed my melancholy and moved in close and asked what was on my mind.

"I don't have anyone to share this with," I said. I knew Gene would have loved South Africa. He was so curious about everything and he had always said the best things about life are the first-time experiences. The second best thing is helping someone else experience it. Living is sharing, he believed.

"I wish I could share this with Gene," I said. "It feels like my life has come to a close."

Dawn stared right at me and said, "You're not done yet, lady."

≈

"What do you mean? A lot of sixty-year-old women spend the rest of their lives alone," I said.

"Haven't you noticed that young man who is hanging out near you all the time?" she asked.

"I know. I have noticed," I said. Earlier in the evening, I watched Frik ambling across the room. He was so tall, nearly seven feet, and I thought he looked like a big ostrich with his slow gate—and yes, I noticed him.

"But why me?" I asked Dawn. "The other gals are younger. Why isn't he paying attention to them?"

"Your life is far from over," she said.

~ 10 ~

Zululand

I felt many moments of loneliness and emptiness in the days and nights I spent in South Africa, but I didn't feel a single moment of regret. Safari had been exciting and more spectacles, unlike any I had imagined, lay ahead.

We traveled through Kruger and eventually landed at a dock where we boarded a boat that was bigger than a pontoon but, like a pontoon, was open on the tops and sides. We wore safari garb, khaki pants and shirts, sturdy walking boots, jeans and hats to protect us from the sun. The last morning in the park, we schooned along a deep waterway—it might have been the Crocodile River—in search of hippos bathing in the river. The water was murky, not clear, and probably alive with crocodiles.

Down river, we spotted a herd of hippopotamus. They seemed docile, but one in the herd was more aggressive and came up out of the water several times

~

and bellowed at us. He seemed dominant and might have been the bull.

Our guide warned us to avoid attracting attention. He said they can charge and they can run fast.

"Just watch," he said. "Don't try to stand up or make sudden moves."

He explained that hippo meat had become a delicacy and the number of herds had declined to a dangerously low level. The sale of hippo meat is illegal, he said, but sales are active on the black market. The ban on elephant's ivory tusks had made hippo teeth more valuable to poachers.

The hippos, even the young ones, were enormous and it was surprising to see that their skin had a pink tinge to it, like pigs on a farm. They looked dark because they roll in the mud or wallow under water to keep cool and protect their hide from burning in the sun, but I could see pink in the flaps of their ears and around their eyes. They looked like huge barrels floating in the water and they'd go down in the river and rise up with their massive heads and open mouths. Even their teeth were huge. But I didn't think of them as ugly or awkward. I found them to be amazing and beautiful in the way they adapt to their own environment. They repeated their ritual over and over again: wallowing in the mud and soaking in the water. They even give birth under water, the guide told us, and they don't venture out on land to graze until after sundown.

It felt like they were watching us while we watched them. They were fascinating, but I started to have an anxious feeling, wanting to get back to shore, wondering what Frik was doing. He had waited on shore to help dock the boat when we pulled up and clusters of native women had gathered around him. The women were chanting and dancing in cloth skirts with beads rattling and clicking around their necks and ankles. Their skirts were dyed in yellow, green and orange colors and wrapped to come up between their legs, like diapers.

They were very tribal. They bared their bodies and unmarried women were topless. Their breasts bounced when they danced. I wasn't used to seeing women dancing around topless and with Frik standing there, I felt embarrassed.

They were primitive in lifestyle and yet they were performers; hopeful, I was sure, that tourists would reward them with money. I didn't realize it at the time, but their tribal exhibition was simple and modest compared to what we would see that night in Zululand.

The day was sunshiny and bright and we drove awhile before stopping at a roadside village for sandwiches. Drivers knew the area and knew where to stop so we could get out and laugh and talk and lunch at outdoor tables.

By then, we had headed toward Durban and the Indian Ocean, leaving the adventures of Kruger Park and safari behind. We had seen the Big Five, plus water buffalo, hyenas, antelopes, giraffes, zebras and leopards and we were off to Zululand.

The Zulus, the largest tribe in South Africa, were known early on for being fierce and violent descendants of King Shaka, the Warrior. They are peaceful now, but they still hunt and kill their own game. We watched them make their hunting weapons in an open area, like an outdoor arena surrounded by a circle of one-room grass huts, their homes. They worked around fire pits, heating and hammering metal into sharp tips for their spears. Some tribesmen were older, some were younger and in the tribe, as in any group, there was an array of silhouettes. Men who threw spears were strong, chiseled and flexible. Their legs were strong from running and jumping and tribal dancing. Especially the young ones, the hunters, had a very muscular stature. Later, to entertain us, they staged a spear-throwing contest involving the tourists. Spears were heavy and hard to handle and the white guys couldn't throw them very far or very well, but the Zulu men were accurate and strong and hit the target every time. I could see they'd have the strength to run a spear through anything or anyone.

I loved seeing village women in their native garb and I got used to seeing the young, bare-breasted ones. Their costumes reflected their status, married or unmarried, available or taken. Married women wore elaborate headdresses that were reminiscent of the days when I wore stylish and fashionable hats, but mine didn't carry such heavy traditions. Theirs were part of their daily dress; mine were rarely worn. I remember wearing a designer hat with a feather when Gene and I were married and I wore a hat to my son's funeral at Windsor Presbyterian in Des Moines. It seemed respectful to me.

I had probably collected fifty hats through the years and after Scottie and Gene died, I put them in a huge box for the estate sale. I needed to part with a lot of my history and when I saw the Zulu women in exotic, hand-beaded headdresses, I realized I wasn't the only woman who loved hats. The tradition goes back hundreds of years and for them, hats show status.

Tribal women also made beaded bags and bracelets and belts and wood carvings and colorful pots and they sat outside their huts to sell their handiwork to us. It was like an open marketplace, a center of commerce in the village. We were told that because of their warrior history, Zulu women pass their wares by using their right hand only. They hold the palm of their left hand under their other arm, a meaningful custom that shows they have no hidden weapons and the buyer has nothing to fear.

We were also told they use color to communicate a message of love, grief, jealousy or other emotions. Young Zulu girls use the vocabulary of colorful beads to send sweet or angry thoughts to their intended loved ones. Zulu tribes still thrive in the bush throughout South Africa, we learned. But in this particular village, natives were hospitable and had become somewhat commercial.

Our housing was beyond the main camp in modern accommodations that resembled the native huts. I was led to mine along a stone path by an elder, a small and shrunken member of the tribe. He wore a skirt of animal skins and loops through his ears and he had a body odor that was horrific. There is no electricity or plumbing in their camp and his smell was overpowering. He carried my luggage and placed it in the room and I covered my nose after he left because the odor lingered.

What must we have smelled like in the pioneer days? I couldn't help but wonder. People then weren't used to regular bathing. Maybe they got used to the odor, like the Zulu seemed to do.

The smells in the village that night were different, though also visceral. After dinner in the lodge, we were led back to the village for a powerful show of tribal culture. The communal space was open, the air was cool and scented with smoke from fire pits. We gathered around on bleacher-style seats, like spectators.

For the Dance of the Warrior over open fire, tribesmen wore no shirts and were draped in heavy beads and necklaces and looped earrings, leather and fur and feathers. They greased their skin with animal fat and their bodies reflected the firelight as they danced. The music—I think it was called Maskanda—started with drums and chants that were earthy and primal and said to be coming from the souls of men who had walked long miles to meet their warrior Chief. Their dance was an immensely raw and powerful marriage of tribal traditions, chanting, rituals, rhythms, drumbeats and dance. I had never in my life experienced anything so sensual.

What rose up within me in response to their dance and the sounds and the physical movement of the athletic and muscled Zulu men was primal. It's almost as if they held a public orgy. When I was young, I went to concerts and got excited over the band and the performers, but it was nothing compared to the Zulu dance. A tribesman pulled me to my feet to join the dance and I did, trying to follow the moves and the beat and slap my feet against the ground, like he did. I don't know that I'd ever felt so much raw sensuality in my life—the fire, the garbs, the colors, the dancing, the beads and furs, the drums.

Afterwards, Frik took my hand and led me back to the bleachers. He put his arm around me. I felt at that moment that I had feelings for him, a strong instinct from the depth of my aloneness, a feeling that made me think that moment marked a turning point on the trip. He later walked me to my unit. He held me by the arm, like a European gentleman.

He opened the door to my room, switched on the light and reacted. There was a huge scorpion in the middle of the room and I'd swear it ran toward us. Its body was huge and its legs shot out, like a crab, but crabs move slowly and the scorpion scurried right at us. Frik bolted through the door and smashed it under the sole of his hiking boots. I could hardly look at the scorpion with its legs and pinching claws and forked tail shaped like a devil's tail, probably poisonous.

"I'm not going to sleep in this room," I said.

"I killed it," Frik said. "It's dead."

He assured me there was no danger. He was kind and caring, never crass, and at that moment in my life, kindness was all I could handle. He left me alone in the room and through another dark night, I lay anxious and sleepless, worrying that someone or something would crawl in one of the little windows in the hut. My thoughts returned to home and the luxuries of our house on Bay Hill. In South Africa, I saw what people do to survive and I was amazed at what they do without. I had had everything. I knew that. My life had been sophisticated and privileged and large. I owned more material possessions than I needed and more than most people accumulate in a lifetime. In contrast, especially compared to the lifestyle I saw in this village, my homes and my lifestyle had been bigger and much grander than was necessary. Here, I became aware of the minimal. And I spent another night alone in the dark with only my thoughts as company.

I remember thinking, *I wish Frik was here.*

Last Night in Durban

With safari over, the last leg of our trip stretched out in a way that seemed less adventurous and more placid with tours through botanicals and market places and sightseeing in Durban. But I felt no peace. I had started to feel obsessed.

The agenda Matt had planned led us to the city of Durban and the Beverly Hills InterContinental Hotel, pure luxury on the Indian Ocean. The climate was sub-tropical—perfect in November!—and beaches were clean and gorgeous. The history of the shoreline, as told to us, was legendary: a British adventurer had befriended Zulu King Shaka and was richly rewarded for it. Henry Francis Fynn, a Brit, helped Shaka recover from a stab wound he had suffered in battle. As a token of gratitude, the Warrior King granted Fynn a strip of coast one hundred miles in depth. The story seemed like the fairy-tale friendship of the Lion and the Mouse, a lesson from childhood.

My room at the InterContinental overlooked the Indian Ocean and the soft, fine sand of the shore, a whiter sand than I'd seen before. The bath and bed-room were done in a deep mahogany. The bed was raised on a dais, like a throne surrounded by a railing. Steps led down to a sitting area with a sofa and chairs where Frik would later visit.

We were to fly to Cape Town before leaving South Africa and Frik would not be with us after this one night in Durban.

As I wandered around the gardens our last day in Durban, I watched for Frik and I saw that he was watching me.

What is wrong with me? I asked myself. *This is no time to think of romance.*

I followed the stone paths in the elegant garden and was surrounded by exotic plants I couldn't name and had never seen, not even in high-end florist shops in America. The scent was like a thousand perfumes. I wandered, watching Frik mingle with other guests, doing his job, until he caught up with me along a gar-den path. He asked if I'd like to go with him to have a cup of tea.

We went off alone into a courtyard cafe in the gar-dens and we talked over hot Rooibus. The scene was like a painting with florals all around—the African tulip trees in bloom and the shrubs with creamy white and fragrant blossoms. The tea and the conversation felt good and warm and Frik was so handsome. I loved to listen.

He would be leaving us—we would be leaving him—when we flew to Cape Town the next morning. I knew that, but what I didn't know was the suspense and anxiety our last night would hold.

Our group was scheduled to have a semi-formal dinner, a departing celebration. We had been outfitted in casual clothes for travel and we, the women, decided to dress for dinner. The hotel shuttled us to Gateway Mall in Durban where the sophistication of the stores and the high fashion we found in designer boutiques was dazzling.

"You've got to get something wonderful," Dawn said. She'd been nudging me toward Frik, coaxing me along the whole trip. "Get something that looks feminine. Something that really looks like you."

We decided on a black linen tunic with a stand-up collar. Buttons ran down the front of the jacket and side pockets were sewn into the seams. I bought a silk scarf and gorgeous earrings to dress it up. I found a pair of strapless heels with mesh treatment and stitching on the toes. It's odd—the things we keep as symbols from the past. I still have the shoes as I tell this story years later. Sometimes I notice those shoes on the closet shelf and I look at them and pick them up and hold them and turn them in my hand and remember that last night in Durban. I haven't been willing to give them away. Maybe I never will. Maybe someday they'll go to Shannon.

I wore them when we went to dinner and I felt a little more like the woman I had been. Before dinner, I started to organize my luggage for the next morning's early flight to Cape Town and I had bought so much in the marketplaces and the mall that I overstuffed a suitcase and broke a latch. I mentioned it to Frik.

"I can fix that," he said.

"You don't have to do that for me," I said.

"That's why I'm here. Would you like me to fix it?"

"If you can," I said.

"I can fix anything," he said.

He came to my room and sat on one side of the sofa the size of a love seat, upholstered in a soft, leafy green tapestry. Brass lamps were on each side and the setting was continental, tastefully done so anyone from any country in the world could feel comfortable there. I settled into a spot next to Frik, watching his big hands in motion as if it was magic. My heart was going and going and going, nine-hundred and ninety-nine miles an hour. He was exciting to look at, exciting to have in my room.

What am I doing? What am I thinking? What is he thinking?

He fixed the latch and sat back, relaxing on the sofa. We talked and he touched my hand.

Oh, my God? I thought. *What do I do now? Is he going to touch me?*

He stood and said he'd see me at dinner and he left my room.

Our dinner table was set in a wonderful restaurant at the edge of the sea. I hoped Frik would join us and I hoped there'd be an open chair next to me. By this time, everyone was making sure of that.

"He really cares about you, Barb," Billie Ray said. "He's really good looking and he's taken with you."

What she said seemed like a fantasy, but I was buying into it. I enjoyed looking at Frik and listening to him and I knew he felt disappointed that we were going on to Cape Town without him. I felt sad, too.

Everyone said their good nights before returning to their rooms at the end of the evening and Frik singled me out.

"Will you sit with me?" he asked. "Will you sit with me and have some tea?"

We walked through patio doors to an open courtyard with a small round table, a sofa and two over-stuffed chairs. Frik sat in a chair, filling it with his size, and I sat on the sofa, facing him. We could see the Indian Ocean lit by bright spotlights that scanned the landscaping and trees and shined on waves that rolled in and washed over the sand on the shore.

We talked until after one o'clock in the morning. By then, he had heard about my losses, my grief and my business ventures. And I knew about the business of his life, his two sons who lived with him and with their mother (his former wife) who lived in the house next door. Like so many people in South Africa, he was entrepreneurial and held several jobs as a guide, a driver, a landscaper and gardener. I knew he had a girl-friend and he lived with her.

What's going to happen?

I couldn't guess. I couldn't process what had already happened and what was happening then. I had come there from a life I believed was over. A life where I had been loved and privileged and filled with travel to exotic places. Yet I had never seen this ocean or the constellations of the South African sky and in it, the Northern Cross cluster of stars. There we were, Frik and I, on a little patio in a warm, ocean breeze and I looked up at the sky, at heaven. What I saw was completely new and the experience felt surreal.

How can I be here under an entirely unknown sky on an ocean I'd never seen with someone I never knew existed? I wondered.

I felt I had been lifted out of the life I'd been strug-gling to survive and set down again in a soft place that was so fresh, so new and so amazing.

It was life itself that amazed me more.

"I need to go," I said, finally. "I need to get some sleep before the flight in the morning."

Frik walked me to my room and waited with me while I slid the key into the door. I was nervous and anxious.

Is he going to kiss me?

He gave me a hug and said good night and walked away.

Oh, my God. He's gone. I'll never see this guy again, I thought.

He stopped in the corridor. He turned back before I went into the room.

He said, "Would you like to have breakfast in the morning before you go to the airport?"

I was thrilled. I was infatuated. To have breakfast with this man who was so beautiful and kind and considerate of me.

I showered after Frik left and I dressed in the fluffy, white robe provided by the hotel. I was just about to get into bed when I heard a knock on the door at two o'clock in the morning.

"It's Frik," he said.

I opened the door in my robe and there he was.

"I'm going to try to make it to breakfast in the morning, but I want you to know one of the guests in your group is not well. I'm taking him to the hospital," he said. "I'll try to be back for breakfast before you leave."

He won't make it! I thought.

I went to bed, but didn't sleep. To think I'd never see Frik again made me sad. Dawn and the others called early in the morning, asking me to join them for breakfast.

"I want to, but Frik invited me to have breakfast with him," I said. "I'm waiting to see if he makes it."

Dawn started to giggle, like a teenage girl.

≈

"I'd go to breakfast with that guy, too," she said. "What happened last night?"

"Nothing happened," I said. "He helped me with my suitcase and we talked about going to dinner. And he left."

* * *

He did call. He did make it to breakfast the next morning. We walked through the dining room together and all my friends at the table said, "Good morning, Barb! Good morning, Frik!" as if they'd had an expectation.

We settled in the bright sunshine on an oceanside patio and the sea and the setting were as beautiful as they had been the night before.

"How about taking a walk?" Frik asked.

We followed a stone path along the ocean, just talking.

I felt small next to him and I loved the feeling because I'm not small. I'm six-feet tall and the only other man who ever made me feel small was my son.

Safari had been wonderful, but Frik was the wonder at that moment. He reached and took my hand and I felt a wave of sadness. He would be leaving me. I would be leaving him. I felt like I was suffering another loss. Not as great a loss, but a loss and deep, deep hurt was just beneath the surface.

～ 12 ～

Going Home

Frik hugged me at the Durban airport and made sure I had his phone numbers before I boarded for the last leg of the trip, a final stop in Cape Town. I watched him drive away. I thought, *I'll never see him again.* I must have said it out loud.

"You'll see him, you'll see him," Dawn said. "Call him up when you get home."

"He lives in South Africa," I said.

We flew to Cape Town and it was as cosmopolitan and beautiful as any city I'd ever seen. There was a vitality in Cape Town in the exotic shops and restaurants and the cuisine was heavy with spices. The city had grown beneath the Table Mountain range and it laid along miles of shoreline on the ocean that looked more teal and azure than blue. Neighborhoods were known by colorful names, like Devil's Peak, Signal Hill, Table and Bantry Bay. We strolled along cobbled streets, past shops and cafes and in one neighborhood,

～

working-class cottages were painted in lively colors, lime green, yellow and pink.

But my focus had changed. The landscape didn't hold the same romance for me—not that I went there for romance. In the final days of the trip, Frik would not be with us and in his absence, I felt an emptiness again.

We, the group, dined on the Indian Ocean in Cape Town with a man named Norman as our guide. During dinner, Norman's cell phone rang.

"Barbara! It's for you," he said. He handed the phone to me as if it was a gift. "It's Frik."

I felt a rush, like panic. Frik tried to call on my cell and couldn't get through since my phone hadn't been converted to international access. He called Norman's number to reach me.

"Do you mind if I use your phone, Norman?"

He didn't mind so I excused myself and left the table.

"What are you doing?" Frik asked.

"Thinking about you," I said.

"I'm thinking about you," he said.

He was home in his garden in Pretoria, working on a wagon, fixing a wheel.

I was so glad to get the call, I ran out on a pier—and you won't believe this—I took hold of a pole and swung around it like I was a ten-year-old. We talked and when I went back to the table, dinner then seemed more wonderful. Everyone was happy for me, glad that I had accidentally found a way out of grief, however it happened and for however long. I slept well that night for the first time in months or maybe all year. The following morning was filled with sightseeing in Cape Town. More botanicals. More markets. A nature reserve. Courtyard dining on the sea. A boat trip to study a herd of fur seals on Duiker Island in the Cape. A climb up the stairs of a lighthouse for a stunning view from Hout Bay.

I wandered around. Everywhere we went, I was thinking. Three more days. There's no one I want to share it with more than Frik.

I borrowed Norman's phone to call him.

"Join us," I said. "If you will, I'll cover your flight to Cape Town."

"I can't," he said. "I have obligations."

I felt sick.

"How much time do you have at Johannesburg Airport?" he asked.

From Cape Town, we'd fly back to Johannesburg where the trip had begun and where it would end. After a four-hour layover, it was home to America from there.

"If your flight's on time and if you can arrange it, I'll wait for you in the hotel across the drive from the airport," he said. "It's less than a block from the airport's main entrance. I will wait for you."

* * *

All I could think about after that call was getting back to Johannesburg to see if he was waiting.

"Go! Go!," the women in the group urged when we landed. "You have to meet him! You have to! We'll take care of your luggage. Take your ticket! You know the gate."

I touched up my lipstick with a compact from my purse and I ran and ran and ran through the airport entrance, out into the drive and through a mass of cars and cabs and people hauling luggage into the hotel.

I was afraid. Fearful that he would be there and fearful that he wouldn't.

What if he's not waiting for me? What will I do if he is? I don't want to be disappointed or saddened again in my life.

My emotions were running as fast as I was when the sliding glass doors at the hotel opened and I went through, looking to the right and the left, scanning the lobby filled with travelers and guests. I saw the back of a sofa in the lobby area and I could see Frik's head and shoulders above the sofa's crest. I rushed around to the front and when he stood up, he reached out and as tall as I am, he picked me up off my feet and that's when he kissed me.

It was a beautiful kiss and what do I say about it? I don't know. It was something I hadn't experienced for a very long time. I had been married twenty-five years and Gene had been sick at the end. We had kissed, but not like that, with another man in another country.

"Let's leave," he said. "We need to move to a more private place."

We found a small sitting area on a patio and few people were around. We talked and held hands then walked along the ocean shore for three hours before my flight.

"I think I love you, Frik," I said. He looked at me, surprised.

"Don't get nervous. There are all kinds of love. It's important for me to feel it," I said. "I need to feel that I can love something or someone and it happens to be you."

He was fine with that.

Time got down to the wire and my flight home would be boarding.

"Come to America," I said. "Just come."

I told him I had many luxuries to share and no one to share them with. I wanted to stay in that moment. I knew I had all the material possessions that are associated with a good life—why couldn't he be part of it?

I still remember nights in the house on Bay Hill when I'd go to sleep and pat the back of Gene's head and think how grateful I was that he was in my life and hoped that he would always be with me. A little doubt would creep in that those moments would go away. Everyone knows loss is imminent, always on the horizon, but it's not something to dwell on. So I'd crawl into bed and look at Gene and think I'm so lucky and I wanted to keep it that way forever, but that wasn't possible.

If I'd been rational, I would have known I couldn't put my life back together again, but I wanted to. I was grasping, but I didn't think I was grasping. I didn't think of complications with Frik. I didn't address reality. I only thought, *My God. He can fix my life. He can fix me. It'll be a good life for him.*

I probably could have stayed, but I decided I needed to go home.

Frik helped me get back to the airport and we worked our way through the traffic and the crowds. A guest in the hotel, a young man about twenty, shared the elevator with us and he could see that Frik—who was wrapped around me—was Afrikaan.

"I'm trying to get this man to come to America with me," I said. "Wouldn't you do that?"

"In a heartbeat!" the guy answered. "I'd go to America."

My friends had left my luggage at the security desk, not knowing whether I'd make it back for the flight. Frik and I claimed the luggage and ran toward the gate, laughing and running, out of breath. Everyone was moving through the boarding gate—Dawn and Phyllis and Billie Ray and Matt and Kay—and they had saved a place for me in the line. They thanked Frik and hugged him and he kissed me and said goodbye. Then we were gone and so was he.

"You're lucky, Barb," they said.

" You'll see him again," Billie Ray said.

"He lives in South Africa and I'm going back to America, for heaven's sakes," I said.

We talked about the trip on the flight home and all the ladies told me they thought Frik was wonderful. I felt good that he had given me a kiss and said he cared about me. That was the first time that year that I didn't feel desperately alone.

We landed in Atlanta, then flew on to Des Moines. We said our goodbyes again and swore we'd stay in touch and everyone said, we love you, Barb. Then they went off with the families who had picked them up to take them home.

I had sent postcards to my family while I was away, but we were scattered geographically. After Gene and Scottie's funerals, Tania had moved with the kids to Arizona and the rest of my family had gone back to the Carolinas, California and Missouri. They loved me, I knew, but they'd returned to their homes and to living their lives, as they should. I tell people that when you've suffered a great loss, the death of loved ones, you have to walk the walk alone. I was very aware of that harsh reality. Everyone has their own lives, not mine.

I could have called Pat who had worked with me through the years and was a loyal friend or I could have called Shelley. But I felt that would make me seem dependent and needy. I had always been an independent business woman and I'd never asked anyone to take me to the airport or pick me up and I didn't ask then. My solitude was self-imposed, like it had been on many nights during the trip. I needed to go home by myself and be by myself.

I'll see them after I get settled in, I thought. I need to learn to maneuver by myself.

It was November, cold and bleak in Iowa. A little snow was on the ground and trees were without their leaves. I'd come back into reality after an escape that seemed like a time warp, like time travel. I wheeled my luggage to the parking lot where I'd left the car for fourteen days. It started with no problem, but it was cold.

I took the interstate home to the house on Bay Hill where Gene and I had been so happy. I passed Des Moines Country Club where we had played golf so many summers and had danced so many times on that ballroom floor. Gene was a great dancer!

Everything had emptied—the tennis courts, the pool, the fairways that had changed from vibrant green to a dormant brown. But I could see in the distance that the clubhouse was dressed for the holidays. Christmas lights were lit and greenery decorated the entrance gate. The greenery was a symbol, a reminder that Thanksgiving and the holidays were coming, and that gave me a sick feeling in the depth of my stomach.

The holidays would be filled with parties and festivities and families. I knew I'd be invited and with the escape to South Africa over, I'd have to force myself to

Big Guy With a Baby Face. Scottie was so kissable and just a big kid with his kids, Grant and Shannon, his wife, Tania, and his mom, me.

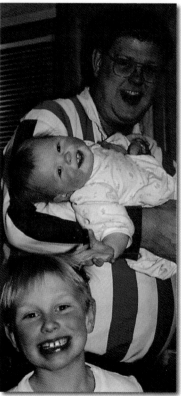

Johnston Little League 2001

The Team. Scott is the tall coach in the back. Grant is front row, second from left. The winners are the Johnston Little League team. They honored Scott with a memorial at the ballpark.

Game Day. The biggest Iowa Hawkeye fan ever with his buddies. (left). Scott and Tania played in the Amputee Golf Tournament Scottie organized in honor his forever friend, Scottie Moore, an amputee (right).

All in a Row. Scott and his business associates lined up before a Las Vegas flight.

Boone County Railroad. Gene and I took Grant on a day trip after his dad died (above). Grant chugged along in his blonde bangs and his Harry Potter glasses on the train ride.

Easter Sunday. The Easter Bunny showed up for Grant and Shannon on our first holiday without Scottie. It was hard.

Gene & His Girls. Shelley and I kissing our favorite guy at a party. Gene was sick by then (above). Here he is with the smile that never faded away (right).

Grandpa & Shannon. Shannon loved her Grandpa Gene. After chemo, he was very sick and Shannon cheered him up with a big kiss on the lips.

The House on Bay Hill. We were so happy here. You can see the window in Gene's favorite nook (above). And who wouldn't love the desert view and the sky above our Arizona home (below).

What a Life! Relaxing on an outdoor deck in Vail after a day on the slopes with Gene.

My Handsome Husband. Gene was a great dancer! Here we're dancing at a party for our pal, Sunnie (above). Gene in Prague in his ancestral country (left). Enjoying our London business partner, Franz (below).

Frik in his native South Africa. He was a kind and charming companion. And he spoke in that wonderful accent!

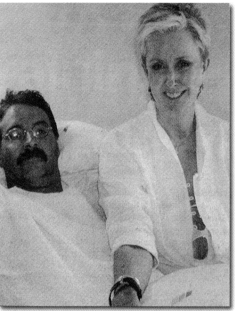

In the News. With Frik at Empangeni Medical Centre after the hijacking that made headlines. Photo: Courtesy *Zululand Observer*.

Intercontinental. Frik faxed handwritten letters from South Africa.

South African Hide-Aways. Accommodations range from comfortable and cozy (above) to one-room huts, tribal homes in Zululand. The exotic hand-beaded headdresses worn by married Zulu women show style and status.

hide my hurt. There is no wrong or right way to grieve, but I didn't know my own way. *I wish the holidays weren't coming so soon*, I remember thinking.

I thought of Scottie. Thanksgiving was such a big event for him that he'd start preparing weeks ahead of time. He'd plan the menu, buy groceries and round up the guests, making sure Jack's sisters and their families were included. He bragged about his special oyster dressing and it reminded me of my two brothers who are sure everyone who comes to their table is well fed. Scott and Tania would spread a white tablecloth over a big Ethan Allen dining room table and set it with their wedding china. Scottie loved Christmas too, and gave Lucky the Golden Lab to Grant the last Christmas he was alive.

I noticed lights in the windows at Kramer's and White's when I turned into Bay Hill Drive. Someone was home in the neighborhood. Someone was nearby and that seemed reassuring. The house felt cold when I went in, but it was beautiful, rich with art and accent pieces, upholstered chairs and gorgeous sofas and rugs in white. I turned up the thermostat and I remember seeing Gene's special nook off the kitchen, his favorite place in the butter-colored chair with a view of the lake through a bay window.

How bare and empty and cold that spot looks without him, I thought.

The message light on the answering machine was flashing and I still had my coat on when I picked up the phone to check messages, wondering if anyone realized I was home.

It was Frik. He had called three times.

∽ 13 ∽

Home Alone

The phone calls made me feel like someone had thrown a lifeline my way and I could escape being alone in the cold. It changed my mental framework to hear messages from Frik, to play his voice on the recording and know someone cared enough to call three times.

I hope you got home safely, he said.

I loved spending time with you.

I think about you and miss you and hope you're safe.

You're probably back home in Iowa. In America.

I've got some things I'm doing and some issues I'm resolving.

I'd like to hear from you.

Try to give me a call.

I settled into the house, unpacking and checking kitchen cupboards and the freezer for food. I hated to eat alone. Before South Africa, I'd walk across to the deli at the Hy-Vee Store on the other side of University

Avenue. There was a young waitress there, a single mother, and we'd talk to one another as if we were friends. Sometimes, I'd pick up a sweet potato or a piece of chicken, but meals were a low priority. Having come from a big, extended family in the Midwest, cooking and eating were done in a group and meals were something to be shared. At night, I'd roam around the house feeling an emotion I can only describe as aloneness, and I convinced myself I should reach out and call Frik. Why not?

If it was any other friend, I'd return the call, I remember thinking. *Why shouldn't I call him?*

I picked up the phone and called to Pretoria. Nine hours and entire continents were between us, but Frik answered right away. I loved hearing his voice again.

We talked for probably an hour and I told him if we were to continue our conversations, I'd place the calls. Without international service, calls were very expensive. He gave me time frames when he'd be outdoors working in the garden or barbecuing on the patio. I knew the guidelines were to avoid a conflict. I knew he was living with a woman named Elmien.

I ignored that reality and set the gift Frik had given me in a visible spot on my nightstand. I was surprised and thrilled that he had thought ahead and had brought a parting gift to the airport in Johannesburg. It was a picture frame of dark wood with a lion's head, an insignia of the troop he served in during the Angolan War carved into the crest of the frame. Frik admitted he was proud, though marked, by having served in the civil war that seemed to never end, and he told me how horrible war is and how his troop had slept on the side of the roads, listening to the rumble of tanks, never knowing if they'd wake up and be alive the next morning. No one I knew personally had been so intimate with war since my dad fought in World War II.

For days and days, I'd move through the house or sit at the edge of the bed with the phone at my ear and I'd look at the gift Frik gave me. It wasn't just a bracelet or a souvenir from a shop. It was meaningful. He put thought into it and I put his picture in the frame.

The wonderful talks and romantic calls we made kept my spirits up and made me believe he cared. I felt I was important to someone and was not totally cut off from life as long as I had an escape through the phone. I knew it wasn't rational, but when I didn't talk to him, I felt myself going back into a dark place, a cold and sad place in my mind.

We talked several times a day and within weeks, I had spent fifteen-hundred dollars on phone calls. I started to think, an airline ticket would be less expensive. I can fly there or fly him here.

But I knew about Elmien.

"I don't do this, Frik," I finally said. "I'm not the other woman in people's lives. It's not how I live."

"I'm going to make some changes," he said.

⁓

We didn't talk for a few days after that. Then he called.

"I did it," he said.

"What do you mean?"

"I did it. I moved out. I'm over at my folks' house. I told Elmien it hadn't been working between us and I needed to move out."

He had made a decision about his personal life and we both felt good about that. The spirit of everything changed for me with that news. I could call when I woke up and before I went to bed at night. After that, I'd wake up at two o'clock in the morning and feel I wasn't alone when I heard his calm, affectionate voice on the phone. We started to talk about him coming to America.

I look back on those times and honestly believe Frik cared about me. But he also loved the possibility of thinking he could come to America. Besides the telephone affair, making plans and talking about the future, thinking there was such a thing as a future for me, was exhilarating. It was hopeful. Whatever his motive and whatever mine, I didn't care. Yet Dawn's reference to Frik echoed in my mind: *That young man.* I remembered when she talked about him in South Africa, Dawn said *that young man.*

Frik may not have realized my age at that point. I wasn't sure of his, but I knew he was significantly younger. We were separated by twenty years, but I didn't talk to him about it and he didn't mention it to me. In European cultures, age differences are less important than in America, I told myself. The issue never came up in phone calls, but it surfaced in my mind. I questioned myself again and again.

What am I doing? Why am I doing this? Is this right? Am I just an old fool?

If I'm honest, I confess that I justified every conflict in my mind, though it's clear now that it was like a teenager's summer romance; it couldn't work. Now that I look back, the distance helps make sense out of all that I tried to hang onto in desperation and all that I couldn't see because I was too close to it.

I had refused medication and counseling after Scottie and Gene died and, trying to be strong, I probably didn't realize the mental condition I was in. The fantasy became the narcotic, the obsession with phone calls at strange times of the day, an addiction. The connection made my sorrow seem less and I believed, like an addict, I needed it.

Finally, I said, "Frik, I'm quite a bit older than you."

"Who cares? What difference does it make?"

"Then, get your Visa. Come to America. I'll help you get a ticket."

I decided that would be a Christmas present for both of us. Alone with him during those late night conversations, I let myself imagine meeting him at the airport and that fantasy moved our plans forward. One night, he called from the road. He held security clearance and that night, he was driving Winnie Mandela. She was

≈

outspoken and strong and the general public feared her, he said, and it was interesting to be with Winnie and her entourage. No longer the wife of Nelson Mandela, Winnie remained a powerful activist whose history was marked by accusations, from infidelity to ruthlessness and human rights violations. Still, Frik said she was powerful. Loved by some, reviled by others.

Our communication went on and on through phone calls and emails. He'd send pictures and little love letters. He'd write in long hand, then scan and send the letters to me to make them seem more personal. For him, our exchange became a family affair since he had left Elmien and was living at home. He'd say, "Here! Talk to Wouter. I want you to meet my brother." Then he'd put Rita, his mother, on the line and it was fun to talk to her, though she had trouble speaking English.

"You fine, Barbara? We want to see you. How happy Frik is," she'd say. "Frik so happy with you."

Frik drove to Johannesburg to apply for a Visa, according to plan. He called afterwards, angry and dejected. His Visa was denied. American officials were functioning in extreme caution after the 9/11 acts of terrorism and Frik failed to meet their criteria—a sufficient amount of money in the bank to cover his stay; legitimate business interests in America; ties to business or family in his home country to ensure he would return. He was a single man without strong financial footing—unapproved.

"We let Americans into our country every day and we befriend you," he said. "And you won't let us come to yours. Why? We haven't done anything wrong."

It was close to the Christmas season and our conversations felt heavier, not as promising, after his Visa was denied. It looked like Frik would not be coming to be with me in America. He was a man in his forties who had left Elmien and moved in with his parents and he was denied a dream. He was unhappy and he felt weakened, emasculated, I think.

It seemed like the end of that road.

"What do you want to do?" I asked one night.

"I want you to come here."

~

～14～

Expectations

Matt Rosen called and asked me to meet him for lunch at Noodle Zoo, a cute little cafe in a neighborhood strip mall. He chose it just for fun as a reminder of where we'd been. The menu, leather-covered and beaded, was as exotic as a menu can be at a small cafe in the middle of America. Walls at Noodle Zoo were painted in zebra stripes and tables were done in animal prints. It seemed like the right background to reminisce about the trip we'd taken to South Africa.

Matt asked if I'd been in touch with Frik. I said I had.

"How's that going?" he asked.

"Pretty well, I think."

Matt told me he was considering buying property in South Africa. "It's economical to buy there. Maybe you'd have some interest in getting into a piece of property with me," he said.

It was the seed of a thought. I could spend more time in South Africa if I owned a condo there. I realized that Europeans have bought homes on the Indian Ocean and have created a trend—why not Americans? Matt offered to look into it and we agreed we'd start to move toward a shared investment and we'd talk about it in the future.

"Tell Frik hello," he said.

I was getting more and more excited about my return to South Africa, but in the days that followed, plans became complicated.

"Are you serious?" I had asked Frik. "You want me to come there?"

"Yes, I want you to come here."

"What would we do? How long could I be there? Where would we stay?" He didn't have an answer for any of that.

It was exciting to think about going back, but I was familiar with what such a major change would require. I thought of Matt's suggestion to buy property and I started to research South African business ventures, trying to ground the plan in practicality, talking to both Frik and his brother Wouter regularly. They'd pass the telephone back and forth and Wouter became an ally and co-conspirator by telephone.

One night while talking to Frik, I heard water running in the background. It sounded like a distant waterfall.

"What are you doing?" I asked. He said he was stretched out in the bathtub. "I'd like you to be here with me," he said.

We set a January date for my return. I already had my passport. If there was a chance at a new life, I wanted to take it. But before that, I filled a social calendar, seeing friends in Des Moines, accepting invitations and going to brunches and Christmas parties for the first time without Gene. Carol and Paul Knapp's annual party had always been special and I went, all dressed up and thinking I was like some young thing who could run off to South Africa and meet a gorgeous and wonderful man and life could be picture perfect again. I talked openly about my plans, adding to the chatter, and there were people at the party who judged me, I knew. There was an occasional veiled comment and a few questions, like how long has Gene been gone? But I justified what I was doing.

Don't judge my actions until you've walked in my shoes, I thought and sometimes I said it. I buried my son then I walked my husband through his death and that was the greatest gift I could give him.

I had been invited to lunch with a widow's group and had joined them once or twice, but they talked about their pain and their loss and I was determined not to let death define me. It wasn't that I would go to South Africa and never think of Scottie or Gene, but I believed I needed to create a new way to live. If it meant going halfway around the world and forcing something to happen, I felt I had to do it.

Some in my circle, including Shelley, considered the return trip unnecessary, if not foolish. After her dad died, I hadn't been as strong as Shelley had known me to be. I hadn't been there to help her grieve. Plus she was fearful.

"I don't know why you're going back. We need you here," Shelley said.

I told her I'd met some people there and they'd said, "You're alone. Come back and be with us. We'll show you South Africa the way you didn't see it on a tour. You have your mother and your family, Shelley," I said. "And the fact is, I am alone."

The real fact was, I was going to see Frik. Sunnie questioned that.

"I don't know what you're thinking!" Sunnie said. "How can you go to South Africa by yourself? You'll be over there all alone and he could be some weirdo."

"He's not a weirdo, Sunnie," I said. "Other people we know have met him. He's not a weirdo."

Sunnie and I are so unalike. Next to me, she's a miniature. She's barely five-feet-two, and I tower over her in height. But she's strong and she's mighty. She's conservative in style while I'm more flamboyant, but she wears a necklace of tiny tear-drop diamonds that I've told her I covet. The diamonds are linked on a chain and they glitter and glow and if someone asked me, I'd say that's the way our relationship is. There's a link, a bond, that holds us together. She is steady, smart and consistent and that's why it's amazing that a sensible woman like her—or like any woman—would fall into the trap of deciding to chase after romance and invest a small fortune in a man.

There was a time, Sunnie told me, when she went off with a guy after her divorce. She said she spent forty-thousand-dollars on him before it was over and she met and married Roger.

"I don't want you to make a such a dumb mistake," she said.

She kept hammering at me and I said, "Sunnie, leave me alone or I'm going to cry. And what the hell, Sunnie? At least I'd be going down fighting."

Everything Sunnie does is done decisively. So she confronted me and just as fast, she backed off and let me go.

"Okay. Just be careful and don't let it cost you forty grand," she said.

Family and close friends, I've since realized, will confront and say what worries them. They have a vested interest and will speak up. Others simply say, that sounds exciting. Though I questioned myself and my motives the entire time, I shut out voices I didn't want to hear and I listened to those who said, Go! Go! Go to South Africa, Barb. Do something that might make you happy.

It was then in the framework of the holidays, the season filled with expectations, that I went to Knapp's party and, looking for reassurance, I asked Paul a direct question.

"Tell the truth, Paul," I said. "What do you think about a man living with a woman who's twenty years older?"

"I'd do it for awhile," he said. "But if I was sixty, I sure wouldn't want to be poking an eighty-year-old." His wife laughed and told me not listen to him—just pack your bags and go, she said.

A sort of giddiness, a mix of blind hope and excitement and denial—hearing what I wanted to hear and believing what I needed to believe—had helped carry me into the holidays. It was like dancing on ice, with the danger of falling and getting seriously hurt part of every move. But I didn't think I could be hurt any more than I already had.

There was music and greenery and food and festivities all around Knapp's house and at some point during the party, I sat down and started a social conversation with a man named Steve. I had met him before, but hadn't seen or talked to him for a long time. I told him about my plans to take a second trip to South Africa and I listened to him tell me what he was involved in. He owned an international travel agency and as we talked, a realization hit me square in the face.

"My, God," I said. "You're the one who flew my son's body home."

I started to sob and nearly collapsed. He moved close and hugged me to hold me together and console me while I cried and cried, out-of-control at the

Christmas party because, no matter what I had tried to tell myself or where I had tried to go, there was no way to escape reality's incredible pain.

Christmas Mourning

I took the first trip to South Africa six months after Scottie's death, eight weeks after Gene's. Because Gene was immediately diagnosed after Scottie's funeral and was in the final months of his life, I hadn't mourned Scottie.

"Barbie, I can't watch you do this," Gene had said. "I can't stand to see you so sad." So I hadn't let grief consume me until an incident pushed me over the edge.

I had rejected counseling. For many people, grief counseling helps soothe torment. For me, it reopens the wounds. I deal with pain by putting it away in a certain place and visiting it when I'm forced to and yes, that day would come. Until it did, I chose to mourn in my own way which may have been by running away and going to South Africa and taking a lover who was years younger than me. At the time, I thought Frik was gentle and big and strong and he could make me feel safe. I think there was confusion in me about who he really was. *Was I warped because I was drawn to him phys-ically, though his life and vitality resembled my son's?*

The incident at Knapp's party had jolted me but still, I rejected counseling. I felt that the more I'd replay the pain, the deeper it would go. I knew a woman who had gone through grief counseling and cried at every ses-sion for nine months. I refused to do that. I was deter-mined not to sink into sadness and agony. I had to hold on to something. I called Frik and told him everything was arranged.

The plan included Christmas in North Carolina with Dick and Cindy, my big brother and his wife and their family. Their house would be bustling with brothers and sisters, nieces and nephews, daughters and son-in-laws and children, an extended family to help cushion that first Christmas without Scottie and Gene. Two weeks later, I'd fly to Johannesburg.

I debated whether or not I should go to Raleigh or anywhere, but at the time, I debated everything. Nothing I did was done with confidence. Part of me wanted to hide and part of me felt desperate to belong. My brother had invited me because he was concerned and he had been with me through every crisis I'd ever had since childhood. He came to every funeral, includ-ing Jack's, and it was hard for him, but he has a way of pointing out the goodness in life. He makes people laugh and builds a fence against hopelessness.

I'd been to Dick and Cindy's for other Christmases and I knew their home would be alive. There'd be so much Christmas! A giant Fir tree in the living room, Cindy's hand-carved and hand-painted star on top, a nativity scene arranged on the buffet, wreaths, ribbons, candy canes, snowmen and santa clauses everywhere, hot sandwiches and soups in the kitchen, banquets in the dining room and trays of homemade cookies on tables and countertops.

Cindy decorated a guest room for me with a patch-work quilt and pillows and pictures of kids and grand-kids in frames on the dresser. We went to a midnight church service to hear Cindy sing in the choir and she and Dick said they'd take me to watch the Hurricanes whip some other hockey team, probably Canadians. I couldn't believe how much they loved hockey, such a wild and crazy and violent sport when that's not at all what they are.

The flight to Raleigh left Des Moines with a long lay-over in Chicago where the weather was cold, snowy and damp, definitely not pleasant. I felt chilled all the way through, but hopeful and determined to get through Christmas and try to pick up the pieces of life again. Tania had sold the house and sold Scottie's clothes and she and the kids were on the road, driving to their new home in Mesa on Christmas Day. Going to Dick and Cindy's, then on to South Africa to try to build something and see where it would go was an attempt to do what mom had always forced us to do when we were growing up. No matter what happened, she'd let us cry for awhile and then she'd say, "It's time to get out there and rejoin the human race." I was trying. I planned to look into Matt Rosen's suggestion about investing in property in South Africa. A January flight was booked. And Frik would be waiting.

During the layover in the Chicago airport, a call came in on my cell phone. It was Frik, minutes before I was to board for Raleigh and only days before I would board for Johannesburg.

Frik asked where I was and I told him I was practically on my way.

"Don't come," he said.

"What do you mean, don't come?" I said.

The battery on my phone was weak and I scrambled to find an outlet, trying to recharge the phone and trying to understand.

"I'm going back to Elmien," he said.

I found a spot on the floor next to a wall and I plugged my phone into an outlet so I wouldn't lose the connection. I don't think I was in tears, but I was dazed and confused and couldn't believe what I'd heard. If I'd had any hint of that complete turnabout, I might have been less stunned, but I couldn't grasp what he was telling me. I was in disbelief, still on the floor, alone in a public airport like a piece of unwanted baggage that had been dropped and left there. Then Wouter called.

"It's terrible, Barb," Wouter said. "Mom and Dad are upset and Frik is so unhappy. You call him. He needs to talk to you."

↬

Still on the floor, I heard the final boarding call. I had to leave. I had to get on the plane to Raleigh—what else could I do? I followed other passengers to a small plane on the tarmac outside the terminal in the bitter, Chicago temperature. I started up the steps to the plane, shaking from the cold, when my phone rang again. It was Frik this time, not Wouter.

"I know Wouter called you," Frik said. "But it's just not going to happen. I'm sorry. But it can't work." He said he loved me and he was sorry. He was doing what he felt he had to do.

A piece of luggage and a purse hung from straps over my shoulder and I was trying to keep my balance and juggle the phone when it slipped out of my hand. I heard it hit the steps all the way down and land on the cement below. I climbed back down the stairs, going against the stream of passengers and I stumbled and fell down the stairs and hurt my leg when I hit bottom. Desperate to grab what I had wanted to be a lifeline though it had probably never been any stronger than a thread, I literally crawled around the landing pad on hands and knees in the cold, trying to find the phone. Any hope of hanging on to a belief that had held me above water for awhile was beyond my reach and I was drowning again.

That's the moment I started to mourn.

I felt physically sick, bent over and crippled with the pain of death and loss and the horror of my own behavior.

∾

I have betrayed my son. I have betrayed my husband.

I boarded the plane for Christmas in the Carolinas and was mourning my son and my husband truly for the first time. I was mourning the loss of life for everyone, my grandchildren, Scottie's widow, myself, Gene's daughters, everyone. Mourning what was and what might have been and what will never be. I sobbed and sobbed and, though it was Christmas, I know I inflicted my agony on the other passengers, but I couldn't stop. I couldn't hold myself together. I wasn't sane.

* * *

I was thin and confused and in a state of panic when I landed in Raleigh. My eyes, my family told me, looked vacant and glazed. I know I hadn't grieved and everything came crashing down and I clutched my phone as if it was the only thing that could save me. I was cold, physically sick from the avalanche of grief that I had not let take hold until Christmas.

There had always been strong men in my life—my dad, brothers, husbands, son and grandson. I didn't know who or what to be or how to be without one. Most of what happened that Christmas is a blur when I look back, but I remember I felt sick and yet grateful that I was with people who cared. We took a drive from Raleigh to Dick and Cindy's home on the Atlantic and I remember thinking the ocean looked deep and cold and bleak as me. I felt I might go crazy riding in the car and we stopped in towns along the coast so I could get out and walk and take phone calls. Wouter and I talked back and forth.

He said he didn't know why Frik did what he had done and everyone in their family, including his mother, was unhappy. He put Rita on the phone and she actually cried.

"You come, Barbie," she said in fragmented English. "He happy when he talk to you. He happy when you're here. He be okay."

They were apologetic to me, sorry because they knew I cared about Frik and he cared about me. He had stopped talking to them because they didn't support his decision to go back to Elmien. They felt he was throwing his own happiness away. Even Frik's dad, Corrie, encouraged me.

"Just come, Barbara. He will be fine once you get here," he said. "You come to the airport and we will get you."

Finally, Frik called again.

He said he knew I had rich resources and privileges and opportunities in America. He said he didn't want to complicate my life or come up short by comparison. It was like he had fallen into an abyss—he was refused passage to America, he was living with his parents, his sons were shuffled back and forth between one home and another, and his only means of transportation was a car he shared with Elmien. I doubt he could raise enough money for a car of his own.

"Go find us a place," I said. "I'll pay for it. I'll send the money. We'll get a car."

"I'm sorry," he said.

"I suppose I'll never see you again," I said.

"I don't know that."

"Will I ever talk to you again?" I asked.

"I don't know that either."

∽ 16 ∾

The Scheme of Things

*F*rik's last call left a door open in my mind. I started to feel there was a way out of where I was mentally because Wouter and Frik's entire family encouraged me, practically begged me, to make the trip and come back to South Africa. For the next two weeks, Wouter and I conspired on how we could put a plan in place and surprise Frik.

The plan became as grand as a Hollywood movie with Wouter in the director's seat. We convinced ourselves that our plot was not only exciting, but reasonable and good for everyone. To help pull it off, Wouter involved a business acquaintance of Frik's, a woman named Esther who managed the Royale Car Company. Frik had worked with Royale as a driver who transported tourists and visiting dignitaries in luxury cars. She and Wouter were in cahoots, asking Frik to drive one of her company cars to Kruger National Park where he would expect to meet a VIP passenger. We gave the passenger an alias and Frik had no idea it would be me.

"We must get the Mercedes, Barbara. We must get the Mercedes," Wouter said. "We'll rent it from Esther."

Esther agreed and told Frik his passenger would arrive in a white Mercedes Benz E320. Wouter and his dad planned to drive the Mercedes to the airport, pick me up and Wouter and I would cruise on to Kruger, arriving in style for the surprise.

"You'll be together and Frik will be so happy," Wouter said. He was proud of his scheme and he imagined the happiest ending, as romantic as any movie he'd ever seen. But by then, concern was building among my inner circle at home, even though they didn't know my true intentions. I had withheld the details.

"This just isn't like you, Barb," Shelley said. She had known me as her dad's strong and steady partner and her mentor. I had set Shelley up as manager and co-owner of a business, and she felt that I was leaving her on her own after her dad died. Abandoning her, in a way.

"I beg your pardon! I've worked with Barb for over twenty years and this is exactly the kind of thing she does. She always pushes the envelope," said Pat, one of my most important business associates. Pat is a former nun who married Cecil, a former priest. Both joined my companies and worked side-by-side with me for decades. Pat was a committed Merle Norman manager who took on a huge number of tasks, more work than she should have given the problems she had with her health. She had a management sensibility and a vision for where the businesses should go. Cecil is a steady, put-one-foot-in-front-of-the other guy who joined LuSan, my manufacturing company as a product formulator. He worked in the plant, mixed chemical formulas and shipped orders out the door. They, the ambitious and energetic Pat and the steady and low-key Cecil, balanced one another and they were loyal to me. They cared about the businesses, they cared about Gene and they cared about me. The truth is, I wouldn't have been able to grow my companies without them.

There was no question, whatever I chose to do, Pat and Cecil were behind me. Still, Shelley worried, "What if you come home in a body bag?"

I probably could have come home in a body bag and I almost did. Or I could have not have come home at all. By then, I had come to believe we are put on this earth for awhile and for a reason, and when it's time for a life to end, it's time. I had lost the best and if I lost my own life, so be it. It wouldn't matter where.

Besides, I had learned long ago that criticism is like a moving train. Someone gets on, then another person gets on and the train picks up speed and builds momentum. It happens in business. It happens in families. It happens among friends. It's hard to stop it once it gets rolling. Someone finally has to say, Wait a minute! In the end, I put a halt to the criticism and, though anxious and scared, I made the decision to go.

It could be a catastrophe, I knew. I flew out of Des Moines, leaving bitter cold temperatures behind, stopping over in the Miami sunshine, then landing in South Africa's deep heat. None of my clothes fit by then as I was down at least two sizes after months of barely eating. I had shopped for the trip and left home in leather pants and black boots and, in my mind, I'd look like an international fashion plate and not look my age when Frik and I reunited. The last call I got before I left was from Wouter.

"Don't worry, Barbara," he said. "Get on the plane. Dad and I will be there when you land. You're going to be fine."

I put all my faith, all plans for the future, in Wouter's hands.

* * *

In a state of fear and uncertainty, I landed in Johannesburg. Passengers poured out of the plane and I mingled among them, looking around, unsure about who I was looking for since Wouter and I hadn't met. I had only seen him in photos.

What if he's not like his pictures? What if I don't recognize him? What if he doesn't show up?

I started walking toward baggage claim and as hard as I tried, I didn't see anyone I might recognize.

What will I do if I'm here by myself? I wondered. *I could go across to the hotel where I'd met Frik that last night in Johannesburg. How did one kiss get me into this mess?*

There was a crowd around the baggage carousel and I continued to search for a face that could be Wouter's. Finally, my luggage turned up and as I loaded both pieces onto a push cart, I heard my name, not over the loud speaker, but out of the crowd.

"Barbara! Barbara!" There was Wouter, waving his arms over his head and jumping up and down in the group of people outside the stanchions of the baggage area.

"Yes, Barbara!" He shouted. "It's Wouter!"

He was skinny and slight, not at all like Frik, and not as tall as I am. He was full of energy, bobbing up and down like a jumping jack. His dad, Corrie, was with him. And so was Esther.

Wouter was filled with excitement and all three gave me a hug and were very warm and welcoming. I felt alive and energized because these people were happy to see me. They weren't in tune with the pathetic state of my life. They were in tune with my South African adventure and their excitement transferred to me. I felt the choice I'd made was right and nobody back home could understand that, nor did I expect them to.

We walked over to an airport cafe to get coffee and we settled at a small chrome table, starting to get to know one another. Corrie and Esther stayed for awhile, saying what a wonderful surprise we had arranged for

Frik. Then they left and Wouter and I were alone. We decided to stop at a kiosk that rented cell phones with international service. My phone wasn't equipped for that and I felt I needed it so I could phone home. On a dark road in South Africa one night in the future, that phone would save two lives.

Wouter went out to reclaim the Mercedes from the parking lot and pull around in front of the airport to pick me up at the curb. With a little bounce in his step, he loaded my luggage in the trunk and slid in behind the steering wheel.

"You know, Barbara. There's nothing like the sound of a Mercedes engine," he said with a grin. "Let's drive!"

He was like a twelve-year-old kid, driving a Mercedes as if he had been crowned a king. He wore big glasses that looked huge on his narrow frame, but he sat tall behind the wheel of the Mercedes. And off we went, headed for Kruger National Park.

The roads along the way were desolate and dusty and we stopped the first night in a little hotel. We went into a roadside store to pick up snacks and my jewelry—rings and earrings and a watch—attracted the attention of two girls who worked there. Their eyes followed me as Wouter and I wandered through the aisles. When we stood at the counter to pay, they said, "Oooo. Beautiful rings. Gooooooorgeous. Beautiful earrings. Gooooooorgeous."

"You got good woman," they said to Wouter.

Wouter later told me I should remove my jewelry.

"It's just costume jewelry," I said. "It's not real. They're all glass and glue."

He said, "They don't know that."

That moment sticks in my mind because it's when I first realized I was a white American woman alone in South Africa with an Afrikaan man, away from cities and away from a group. I recognized then that my experiences would be different than before. We drove in daylight because there was danger along the back roads after dark and the danger was not from the animals, Wouter said. The danger was from hijackers. After dark, marauders block roads with their vehicles or lay on the roads, forcing travelers to stop. They attack, steal and kill. I hadn't had a hint of that when I was with my group on the first trip and South Africans don't want tourists to know the dark underside of the culture. The remedy was to travel by day and stop at night.

Wouter turned out to be a charming and delightful companion. His laugh was contagious and light as a giggle. He smoked Chesterfields, a strong tobacco that was popular in America thirty years ago. But he wouldn't smoke in the Mercedes, so he'd pull a cigarette from the pack and tuck it above his ear while driving. I felt like I could close my eyes and see the boys of my teenage years in America, guys who rolled up the sleeves on their t-shirts, stuck a cigarette over one ear, and cruised around in their classic cars. Wouter was just as cute.

He tooled along, turning up the car radio and singing out loud, believing he had done a wonderful thing. He was so proud of driving a Mercedes, so proud that I had come back to South Africa on a leap of faith and he had made it happen, so proud that he could do this for his big brother. Frik had once told me that Wouter loved to maneuver things and this, to Wouter, was the grandest maneuver of all.

"I'm so glad you're here, Barbara," he'd say. "I'm so glad."

We slept that night in a modest, but clean and well-lighted motel. I reserved two rooms, paying one-hundred rands each—ten bucks in U.S. dollars. I expected to use my own financial resources on the trip, feeling that it was my journey and I would pay my way. Wouter's, too.

We left after an early breakfast the next morning so we'd arrive at Kruger before noon. The odd thing is, Frik hadn't communicated with me or anyone in his family since he went back to Elmien. When he broke a tie with me, he broke it with his family because they were against his decision to go back to Elmien. Wouter hadn't talked with Frik at all, but through Esther, we knew when Frik expected to meet his passenger. We knew he'd be driving a small red car.

Wouter and I pulled into Olifants Camp ahead of Frik. I was nervous and jittery, but Wouter was confident. "It's going to be fine," he said. "Frik will be so happy to see you, Barbara."

We parked the Mercedes under a shade tree, waiting and watching for the little red car to come through the gate. Wouter got out to smoke a cigarette, then he suddenly jumped back in the car, saying "That's Frikkie! That's Frikkie. I see the car. It's Frikkie!"

What am I going to do now? I had kissed this man once and I'm back in South Africa with the brother I'd never seen.

Frik drove up near us and I remember thinking he was too big for the compact car he was driving. He looked like he'd been stuffed into it and one arm hung out the side window. He stared at us, as if he couldn't figure out what he was seeing parked there under a tree. My heart was racing. I felt like I was coming unglued.

"Get out of the car, Barbara," Wouter said. "Get out and go over and kiss him like you want to see him! Like you care!"

I got out and ran over to Frik's car and leaned in to kiss him. He held his hand up in my face, like a stop sign.

"No!," he said. "Don't do this! I went back to Elmien. I told you that."

I was not so much humiliated as stunned—or maybe humiliation is the right word. I wish I could say that was the worst moment of the night, but it was not.

"I'm trying to build a life with Elmien," he said. "I never dreamed this would happen and it can't."

No one knew what to say or do after that awkwardness and Frik fell into a silence. He was upset and angry with Wouter and he was probably upset and angry with me. Why wouldn't he be?

Finally, Frik suggested we should go into the lodge to get some tea—he believed in having his Rooibos in almost any situation. We carried cups of Rooibos out onto an open porch surrounding our bungalow and Frik looked directly at me for the first time since he'd arrived.

"I never thought I'd see you again," he said.

Then Frik and Wouter left me alone on the porch and wandered out to the road to examine the Mercedes, a wonderful diversion from all the emotion. The picture I hold in my mind is of Frik, who was so tall, bending down to look inside the car and the two brothers oooohing and aaaahing, admiring the Mercedes like it was some sensual woman while I sat alone. They both had cigarettes dangling from their lips as they talked quietly together about the car. I sat in silence, feeling lost again after leaving behind what remained of my life. When they joined me again on the porch, Wouter was talkative, trying to explain what we had done.

"Barbara got this wonderful car and came to have a vacation with you," he said.

Frik was not unkind. "It's good to see you, Barbara," he said. "But I have changed."

It was a long drive back to Johannesburg and since driving after dark wasn't considered safe, we agreed to stay the night. I had reserved two bungalows, each with an outdoor grill and Frik said he'd like to cook. We drove to a general store near the lodge and picked up steak filets and potatoes and squash. I settled again in a chair on the porch, staring out into the wilderness and watching Frik flip steaks on the grill and wondering what to do for the next ten days. I had the Mercedes and a return ticket to America and not a plan in my head.

The air was hot. Good grief, it was so hot. I actually wished for one of South Africa's summer rains. Then Frik came up to me and hugged me and kissed me on the forehead. He stood beside me, looking at me for what seemed like a long time before he spoke.

"I married Elmien two weeks ago," he said.

⇔ 17 ⇔

Married

*T*he sun was setting and the moon was coming up and we could hear sounds of animal calls in the bush, but when Frik said he was married, I felt like I was in the quietest, loneliest place in the world. As a woman who had always believed in character and integrity, I should have walked away right then, but I didn't. I should have taken the Mercedes and driven off, but I didn't.

"Why? Why? Why would you marry Elmien," Wouter needed to know. He paced back and forth the length of the porch, rubbing his hands through his hair. I could see tears on his cheeks and I was crying, too. At one point, Wouter came over and embraced me, then stomped back to Frik, fists clenched like he wanted to hit him. I think Frik cried, too. He sat on the edge of the porch, looking out at the bush, real tense, real silent, not saying a word.

"Why would you have not told your family?" Wouter asked. Frik didn't answer.

The night went on and on and so did the tears. Wouter was devastated. But it seemed like something, maybe the moonlight, finally helped mellow us. The animals were out in the wilderness, but there was a calmness in the South African night that was wondrous and mysterious. I can't describe the effect and the beauty of an African moon, but I understand it the way the author Alexandra Fuller understood it when she wrote that evening in South Africa *brings a kind of careless, extravagant beauty to the world. It is a time of day when...everything about being alive seems more improbable and fleeting and precious than usual.*

The atmosphere was soothing. It was familiar to Frik and Wouter as they and their families had vacationed at Olifants before. There was some comfort in that and eventually, we settled down to share the steaks and potatoes Frik barbecued. Wouter did most the talking and after hours of conversation, he began to accept that his big brother hadn't invited him to his wedding and hadn't told the family about it at all. We were still on the porch until after two-o'clock in the morning, drinking warm sodas we'd bought in the lodge. Finally, Frik said, "I think I'll stay. I think I'll take this vacation with you. I think we'll be together."

Wow! This is what I wanted him to do, I thought. *But how can I rationalize it in my mind? What can I tell myself?*

Frik seemed nervous and anxious, thinking Elmien would try to call. For him, there was drama and there were responsibilities and conflicts and unhappiness and hope for the future. I was an added dilemma. For me, there was no choice. I had made mine.

"I'm going to bed," I finally said. "We have two cabins. Frik, you can make a decision to sleep with Wouter or you can make a decision to stay with me."

I had brought a white, silk robe. In the bush in South Africa, how much sense did that make? But I wanted to be appealing. I took my shower and when I came out of the shower, Frik was lying on the bed.

"Are you staying with me?" I asked.

"Yes, if you want me to."

"Yes, I do."

He sat up on the bed, then stood and said he was going to take a shower. I laid back down, alone and scared to death, asking myself questions I couldn't answer.

What am I thinking? What is going on in my life? Nothing here or at home is what I thought my life would be.

I laid on my side with my arms around a pillow and my back turned toward the bathroom door. Frik came out of the bathroom wearing briefs. I turned his way and looked at a gorgeous man, and he was glistening.

He slipped into bed next to me and laid on his side. He reached and put his arm around me and pulled me close to his chest and his stomach and because he was so tall, it felt like he surrounded me in a cocoon. I felt safe and loved and looked after and the feeling was warm and comforting.

It was one of the best feelings I had had since my life had changed so drastically. That was the night Frik first made love to me.

～18～

The River Road

That one night in Kruger Park changed us. Frik, Wouter and I went to breakfast the next morning and had a wonderful time. The anger and tension and uncertainty between us had lifted and Wouter was happy and giggly again.

Frik started to talk about going to the immigration office with me and trying again to get a Visa. He had decided that if he could get a Visa, he would risk the other relationship, probably as much for the chance to go to America as to be with me. I had a return ticket and two weeks to help make significant change happen.

Wouter stayed with us for a few days and we explored the park, eating and sightseeing and hiking and doing all the things that can be done in that magical, mysterious environment. We stopped one day at a nice restaurant and dined on an outdoor patio. A Blue Jay flew past us and with full force, it flew against the restaurant's window and dropped to the patio floor.

~

Frik leaned over and scooped the bird up and held it in the palm of his hand. He stroked the back of the bird with his fingers, poured a pool of water in his hand and dribbled it into the bird's open beak.

"I think it's going to be okay," he said.

In minutes, the Blue Jay fluttered and shook and flew up into the air toward a Jacaranda tree. I was impressed that such a big man as Frik could be so gentle.

Our days were filled with fun and companionship, but the time came when Wouter decided to drive back to Johannesburg. He took the car Frik had driven to the park and left Frik with me and the Mercedes. Wouter left us, happy and full of zest. He hugged me before he got in the car and said, "Maybe we'll meet again. Maybe you will come and meet the rest of the family."

Frik and I packed and cleaned up the cabin and our conversation was promising and wonderful as we left the park. We talked as we drove, with Frik telling me about his work, jobs he had held, his dreams and the life he shared with Jenny, his former wife, the mother of his sons. He had managed a staff as a director for a national bank near Zimbabwe. The family lived in a beautiful home and the boys were schooled there until peace was threatened by tribal wars and general unrest in the region. Frik felt unsafe on the roads, driving from one bank to another and he ultimately decided not to raise his sons in a dangerous environment. He walked away from the job, sold the home and moved back to Johannesburg where he joined another bank. Though heavily guarded in that job, he was shot at many times while servicing ATM machines. Eventually, he and Jenny separated and divorced.

I listened as Frik revealed fragments of his history, including his dreams and disappointments, and we drove contentedly on the roads through Kruger Park. The conversation would naturally lead to steps we'd need to take to get his passage to America. He'd take his hand off the steering wheel and reach over and pat my hand and say, "I love you, Barbara. And I'm so glad you came back. I didn't think you would."

Does he say he loves me because he wants to come to America? I want to believe he loves me. I wanted to believe I was loved, but I couldn't help but wonder.

When we left the park, we expected to get as far as Johannesburg before dark, but we didn't. I don't know why we were driving at night, though I honestly think Frik took a wrong turn and got lost. There was no place to stay or to go along the road, but I was comfortable, just tooling along, not conscious of any danger. I thought we'd come across a place to stay.

Frik might have been tense, thinking there was danger, but he didn't let on. Finally, he said he'd been driving a long time and he asked, would I mind if he got out of the Mercedes to have a cigarette.

They drive on the left side in South Africa, so his door opened onto the center of the road. I was on the curb side near a ditch and it was very dark out there, wherever we were. Frik left the car lights on and left his door ajar. I watched him walk behind the car and come around to me. He leaned in and gave me a little kiss.

"Do you want to get out with me?"

Then he raised up and I saw a look of terror on his face.

"Jesus Christ! We have to get out of here," he yelled.

My car door was open and he tried to dive over me when all hell broke loose. The first thing I realized was that the windshield exploded and glass shattered and was flying all over. A bullet must have passed me and hit the windshield. The next thing I knew was that blood was everywhere. I was drenched, wet from blood.

Frik's body stretched over me as he tried to get to the driver's seat and reach the door he'd left open. He must have realized one hijacker was coming up on his side of the car because he grabbed for his door and yanked it shut, hitting the shooter and knocking him off balance. If he hadn't, he would have been shot in the face. The gun went off and I think that's the shot that went through me, just above the knee.

I was covered in blood. Frik's blood and mine.

I have never put the whole picture together because it happened so fast and it comes to me in flashes and images of blood and glass and guns and bodies. But clearly, I remember seeing the shooter on my side of the car. He was black and I looked at him and how strange it is that I would have imagined an evil-look-ing man, but he was not. I saw his face and what he was wearing: a tropical print shirt, like a Tommy Bahama. The shirt was unbuttoned and open at the front and I saw his chest, the white of his eyes and the gun in my face. It was square-barreled and silver.

Somehow Frik got upright in the driver's seat. The windshield was shot out and another window was out on Frik's side of the car. Shattered glass and blood were everywhere. He trounced on the foot feed and the car lunged forward, away from the shooters. If Frik hadn't left the engine running, we wouldn't have got-ten away.

They took another shot at him and the bullet grazed his hand and blew the knob off the gearshift. Blood poured from his hand and blood soaked my clothes. I held my leg with both hands and I felt weak and he reached and touched my leg that hadn't been shot.

"Are you alright?"

"They shot me and I feel sick."

"I've been hit three times," he said. "Once through the gut and I don't think I'm going to make it. You have to."

You are not fucking going to die on me! I needed to scream. *You're not going to die on me. You're not going to die!*

I saw the agony in his face and I don't know how he stayed conscious or how we stayed on the road, though we were all over the road and neither of us knew where we were. Frik was passing in and out, but he kept the car moving and I'd reach over and try to take the steering wheel. I was in a panic because I knew he was hurt so bad. I took my blouse off and wrapped it around his hand. I tried to put pressure on his side and he screamed.

"I think I'm bleeding out," he said. His voice was weak. I thought he was dying.

God, I prayed. *I can't take it. I can't watch another man die!*

I went into survival mode and I didn't get sick or faint. In an instant, being nauseous paled in comparison to surviving. Thank God I had rented a phone in the airport, but the file I carried with contacts and telephone numbers was drenched in blood and was useless. Frik didn't have the strength to recall numbers and I didn't know if South Africa had a 911 emergency service. It was pitch black except for our car lights and up ahead I saw a sign. It was a narrow, green sign set high above the road and there were numbers on it. Why I thought I should punch in those numbers on my phone, I do not know, but I did. It was instinct. It was an emergency number and the man who answered had a heavy Afrikaan accent and I couldn't understand him and he couldn't understand me.

I didn't know where we were or what to tell him. I conveyed that there had been a hijacking and we were shot and injured. Then the car veered off the main highway toward a clearing. I saw a dilapidated building that looked like an auto repair shop. Old cars were scattered around on a dirt lot and there was a sign of life in the background, small lights, maybe from windows in distant houses.

"Tell the dispatcher we're on River Road," Frik managed to say. "We were shot on River Road in Mtubatuba."

He said they'd get somebody out there.

Please come. Please come, I prayed. *I don't know if Frik will live until you get here.*

Then I noticed car lights coming toward us on the main road. I thought, *I can stop them. They can help us.*

I honked the horn and Frik grabbed my hand.

"No! No!" He said, trying to stop me from attracting attention.

I must have thought I was back in a cornfield in Iowa, thinking someone would come and help us.

The car stopped. It looked old, like an antique Model-T. Two men got out. One wore short hair and one wore dreadlocks and a beard. They looked at us and the one with dreadlocks reached his hand through a window that had been shot out and grabbed for the keys. Frik hit the guy's hand and stomped on the accelerator and we lunged forward into a ditch and back up onto the main highway again. That's when I heard sirens in the distance, coming toward us.

The ambulance found us and lifted us out of the car onto stretchers and they could see Frik was in bad, bad shape. They tied my leg with a tourniquet and laid Frik out on a bed in the back of the ambulance, but they had no equipment to take care of him. He needed oxygen and there was no hose for the oxygen mask and there was no medication to help him with the pain. I realized then that they were taking us to a public hospital and I knew if we went there, we could come out with AIDS. I told them I was an American and I had resources and I wanted a private hospital. I knew a stomach wound was deadly and there wouldn't be much time before it poisoned Frik's system.

I held his hand and told him he was going to be fine.

The last time I sat at the bedside of someone near death was in my own home in the bay window of the house on Bay Hill Drive. Gene was in a hospital bed and I slept on the sofa in the living room, right next to Gene's death bed. An oxygen tank was hooked up to him and I could hear the machine twenty-four hours a day going whis-ooo whis-ooo. The sound seemed louder than I could stand sometimes because I knew it was barely keeping him alive. I slept little and I stayed by his bed and held his hand and talked about the things we had done together. I knew we were past the point when I would tell him that he was going to live, but I would tell him, like a promise, that he would be alright. He had some fear as everyone who is facing death does. But Gene was never a coward. He was the bravest man I ever knew.

Then silence. Unbelievable silence. That's what happened with Scottie's death, too. Silence. Tania said she woke up in the night and the silence in the room was deafening. It's not just that there's no breathing, it's an absence. It's a silence that is almost too much to bear.

Dear God, you can't let this happen to Frik, I begged. *Help us! Do not let this happen. You've got to help him. I can't survive another death of someone I love. You've got to see me through to the other side of this and then I will live life. I will create some value.*

We were in the back of the public ambulance, afraid and desperate and speeding down the highway toward Empangeni when I heard another siren.

Thank God! Our rescuers had made contact with Empangeni Medical Centre, a private hospital, and we were taken there. They gave me a sedative and what happened then is foggy, but I remember seeing concern on the surgeon's face. He tried to reassure me, but by then Frik was in septic shock. I heard the surgeon say, "It doesn't look good."

∾ 19 ∾

A Woman My Age

A doctor dressed my wounds and sedated me and I was left to sleep in a private room separate from Frik's. I woke before daylight and the first question I asked was, "Is he alive?"

"He's alive," the nurse answered. "He's asking for Barbara."

Frik had survived seven and one-half hours of surgery in the hands of one of South Africa's finest intestinal surgeons who closed twenty-seven entrance and exit wounds in Frik's colon. The post-operative attention was also intense: surgeons and nurses and attendants and reporters and Frik's family, including his young sons. I tended to him at his bedside, cared for him as a buffer from the activity and the chaos of the following days. Looking back on the experience, the reality comes to me in fragments and flashes, like the way I imagine thoughts and feelings return to an amnesiac. The mind is sometimes incapable of understanding everything at once. I was sedated, feeling

∾

unclear and foggy, but when I reach back in time, I remember two incidents that are still jolting. I was at Frik's bedside, holding his hand, when a nurse came in and handed me a phone.

"You have a call from America," she said.

It was Shelley. Shocked. Worried. Tearful. Angry.

The first thing that morning, Shelley had a call from a newspaper reporter in South Africa.

"I could hardly understand him, Barb! All I could understand was that you'd been shot and you were in a hospital."

I hadn't planned to tell anyone in America until things stabilized. I understood why Shelley would be upset, but I was shocked that she found out. We both knew from losing Scottie that if I hadn't survived, trying to communicate with foreign officials and reclaim a body adds to the grief and horror. That reality isn't revealed in brochures or travel books, but Shelley and I had experienced it.

"The reporter wanted to interview me. He wanted my comments, and I didn't know anything," she scolded. "I need to know how you are and when you're coming home."

"How did you know where to find me?" I asked.

I had left emergency contact numbers with Shelley and she first called Frik's parents. They referred her to the medical centre where she got through by telling the nurse she was a family member in America. In doing that, I couldn't help but think of how much she was like her dad who would track down facts and investigate everything.

"All I knew was that you were alive and I couldn't just sit here and not do anything and wait for you to call," she said. "Why didn't you call me? Here's somebody I love and I had to hear you'd been shot from a reporter."

She reminded me that I was her only connection to Gene and Scottie. And she reminded me that in her mind, my return to South Africa alone was irresponsible. That was the word she used, irresponsible.

"It's still playing in my head, it always plays in my head, that when dad was dying, he asked me to take care of you or watch over you. I know how he felt about you, Barb."

I understood, but there were times, and that was one of them, when I felt my family's concerns were more about them than about me.

The next call that came in was from a reporter at the *Des Moines Register*. *The Register* serves the whole state of Iowa, so even Mom's remaining relatives in Emmetsburg would read about me. I knew it would be big news: Women in my circle don't walk around with a bullet hole in their knee. I called Roger.

"Please," I said, "you've gotta do some damage control for me." I turned to Roger because I knew he'd do what was in my best interests and contain the story. He contacted the media and told them I'd talk to them when I got home. "For now," he said, "there's no comment."

The turmoil wasn't yet over. Later, I was back in my room trying to rest when an attractive blonde woman came charging in the door. It was Elmien.

She was a little on the chunky side, but pretty and soft-skinned, like the beautiful skin of the South African movie-star, Charlize Theron.

Elmien had been to Frik's room and Frik told her he was staying with me.

"I want to take him home," she said in a heavy Afrikaan accent. Her voice was not angry, not loud, but gentle and pleading.

"Elmien," I said, "Frik needs to make the choice."

She'd brought a photograph album with her and she opened it to show me a picture of their wedding that had taken place two weeks earlier.

"Look at his face," she said. "He's happy. He wasn't unhappy."

What am I doing? I asked myself. *This lady is devastated.*

She showed photos of her children, a boy and a girl, and Frik's two sons. They reminded me of my grandkids and my thoughts were racing.

How could anyone take a parent away from his children. My son was taken by what I couldn't control. I could control this.

I felt that sickness that comes over me from torment or guilt. It's a debilitating feeling, like a blow to the stomach. I looked at Elmien and I looked at the pictures and I thought, *My God. I shouldn't be here. I should be the one to leave. But I can't. I don't have the personal strength to make that choice.*

I knew I wasn't being the person I needed to be or the person I truly am. But becoming that person again would not happen for a long time.

"I'm staying as long as he needs me," I said.

I consoled myself with something the psychologist said in a counseling session that the medical centre required before we could be released.

"Frik saved your life and you saved his," the counselor said. "If you wouldn't have been there, Barbara, he wouldn't have tried so hard. He's alive because of you and you're alive because of him."

That fed my belief that Frik and I had become bonded in a unique way because, I remembered that in American Indian lore, a person's life belongs to you once you have saved it. I took the psychologist's statement as an omen, as if I deserved to do what I was doing. And I tried not to think of Elmien again.

When Frik was released after seven days in the hospital, I realized we had no place to go, no place to call home. I decided to take him back to Durban to rest on the Indian Ocean, this time at a boutique hotel, The White Shutters, a smaller and more intimate hotel than the InterContinental. We drove all around the region, sightseeing and looking at a few houses, dreaming, until he got stronger. After ten days there, we went to spend time with his parents. I love to think about his family and their house because it was as homey and cozy as any ranch house in America with three bedrooms, one bathroom and a tub that stood on claw feet. There was a sunroom and a simple kitchen with painted cabinets and a cloth curtain that camouflaged the plumbing under a free-standing sink.

The kitchen table was a spotlessly clean Formica with four unmatched chairs placed around the table's edge. The feeling took me back to growing up in simpler times in my small hometown in Iowa during the 1950s when people sat around the kitchen table and shared good food and laughter and conversation. I remember that Daddy sat at the head of our table, Mom sat at the other end, my sister and I were on one side and the boys were across from us. Our table was Formica and our chairs were probably unmatched, too.

Rita, Frik's mother, had a pot of coffee ready for anyone who came in the door, like Mom used to do. Rita simmered a cut of beef in spices and onions and the smell was as wonderful as the pork Grandpa butchered and brought from the farm when I was still a freckle-faced girl in my teens. We always had something wonderful like home-rendered pork chops frying in a cast iron skillet with gravy and vegetables on the side and mounds and mounds of potatoes boiling on the stove.

After supper at Frik's parents, the family, including Frik's sons, gathered in the parlor with furniture that looked not rickety, but modest (so different than the designer-everything of mine.) They didn't own a TV and they entertained themselves with music. Frik played a guitar, Wouter had an accordion, Corrie played a piano and everyone sang.

It was a gathering place. No wonder it felt like it was home, except for one disturbing difference. Their house was surrounded by a huge, wrought iron fence eight-feet tall. No one could get inside unless the gate was opened to them. Some houses had dual fences and hardly anyone goes out at night because of marauders and rapists and murderers. If they do go out, they drive fast and run stop lights they call robots.

When Frik and I retired to his parent's back bedroom, he'd ask me to lay beside him. He'd put his arm around me and be loving me and kissing me there in the house with his parents and his brothers. I could hear them in the next room. It started to enter my mind that this was strange and it was not right for a woman my age to be with a family like his. It wasn't guilt that I felt. It was a growing awareness of reality. It was a situation that made me ask who I was, who I was with and where did I really belong.

We found a place to stay on other nights, then found a lovely bed and breakfast in a Cape Cod style. The grounds were beautiful and we stayed there for more than a week, sleeping late and eating well. Every day, we'd go to Rita and Corrie's for coffee. Elmien phoned Frik repeatedly, but he refused to take the calls. It was me, not her, who was in the inner circle of the family and friends. We were invited to neighborhood parties and pig roasts in somebody's back yard regularly. Their curiosity and interest in the United States was without limit and they treated me, an American woman, like a celebrity guest.

"She knows George Bush! She knows George Bush!" Wouter would say. Because he knew I had an invitation to Bush's Inaugural Ball, Wouter would say, "If you have a problem, call George Bush!"

I loved the warmth of the people I met, but finding a place to live had started to become a problem and charges on my Visa were rising. The conversion rate from rands to U.S. dollars, though favorable, did not always apply. Out-of-pocket medical expenses and many purchases were not subject to the exchange rate. Some of what I paid for was in American dollars, like the lease on the Mini-Cooper which we both loved. We jumped from hotel to hotel, from rented room to rented room. I was burning through a noticeable amount of money, trying to soothe physical and emotional wounds with expectations. Realistically, I started to wonder how we'd put a real life together.

We went back to our rented room one evening after we'd been with Frik's family and friends—friends his age who had young kids the age of his children, the age of my grandchildren. Some friends had babies crawling around on the floor. By then, it wasn't only my family that worried I was acting out of character. I felt it, too.

In my head, I was thinking, *this is not the kind of life I want to have. I don't want babies crawling around on my living room floor. I've already had that.*

"This is not my life, Frik." I finally said. "This is my son's life."

"Everyone loves you, Barbara," he said. But my doubts were creeping in.

The next time we went to Rita and Corrie's, Wouter told me about a reclaimed car sale north of Johannesburg. "Let's go see how much they cost," Wouter said. I wanted Frik to have his own transportation. I wanted him to go home with me, though the process of securing his Visa was not going well. I had contacted Senator Grassley of Iowa and every official I knew (except George Bush!), but it was a rigorous process and the paperwork had not been approved. Frik was getting anxious, actually angry, because he felt America was barring him, like some outlaw. I was still hopeful, but if I had to go home without him, I wanted him to have transportation until I got back. So we all hopped into the Mini-Cooper, Frik and I in the front seats and Wouter crunched into the back, and off we went to the car sale.

We looked at rows and rows of cars and the prices were more than I had in mind. Frik and Wouter walked on ahead of me and when they came back, Frik told me he had made a bid on a car.

"What?"

"Yeah. We bid on that car over there." He pointed to a blue Dodge compact sitting on the lot. It was going to cost sixty-thousand rands which converted to six-thousand American dollars. That total wasn't beyond my reach, but it was against my nature to go out and blow six-thousand dollars without a thought—and they had already done it. Elmien had Frik's car to drive the kids around, and since he'd have to borrow the car or sit around without reliable transportation, I agreed to put up two-thousand dollars. I said I'd co-sign a loan and help him get credit for the balance.

I was nervous that he might be rejected for a loan. And I was irritated. My expenses had started to add up: American dollars for the Mini-Cooper, hotels and restaurants, out-of-pocket medical care, airline tickets, meals and restaurants. Then I'd suddenly bought a car and I felt like everything was closing in on me. My businesswoman instincts kicked in.

You're supposed to be madly in love with this guy, and you won't give him any more money? I said to myself.

I decided some responsibilities had to go with the relationship and I made Frik sign a promissory note for two-thousand dollars. Gene had taught me never to give money away without a signed agreement. You may never see the money again, but the borrower needs to make a commitment, Gene believed. So Frik signed a promise on a little scrap of paper.

Through all that, I was not feeling at all well. It was nearly one year after Scottie had died, then Gene, and what had I done to my life?

"I'm really sick," I finally admitted. I could hardly stay away from a bathroom and contractions in my stomach were so severe, I doubled over in pain.

"We need to take you to a doctor," Frik said.

He drove me to Pretoria and I was so weak, he practically carried me into the clinic. He had been so very loving and I thought, *Thank God for him. What would I do without him?*

He propped me up and helped check me in at the emergency desk. The woman attendant was very kind and lovely. She asked a few questions, then looked at Frik and said, "And is this your mother?"

~ 20 ~

Touchstones

You can only live a fantasy for so long. Art Filean called me in South Africa to ask if I'd be back in time for our quarterly board meeting. The length of my stay was limited in my mind because of that meeting. In twenty years, I had only missed once.

I was absent at the board meeting the day after Scottie died. I prepared for the next meeting while sitting at Gene's bedside. Always the consummate professional, he said, "You can do this, Barbie. I'm going to be fine. You go to your meeting." That was three days before he died.

Strange as it seems now, the constancy of four annual board meetings are a touchstone for me because of the people, the other directors and because of the calendar. Each meeting falls near Scottie or Gene's birthdays or near the anniversary of their deaths.

When Art called to see if I'd make it, my history, my identity and my natural instincts took hold. I knew

Frik and Elmien had talked and he had spent time with her. He would go back to his family, his beautiful boys. I realized that. Besides, I was diagnosed with two bleeding ulcers which required attention. I wanted to see Charlie, the doctor who was with us when Scottie died and Gene was diagnosed. I trusted Charlie.

It was time to go home.

"Yes, Art. I'll be there," I promised.

The last night I spent with Frik was a melancholy one. I would not only be leaving him, I'd leave his family and his country. I knew I could return. But on some level, I must have sensed that day would never come.

* * *

Nearly a decade has passed since I flew out of the Johannesburg airport for the last time. Wouter still calls every now and then.

"When can I pick you up at the airport in Johannesburg, Barbara," he asks with his usual energy. He urges me to come back and he promises that someday he'll come to visit me in America. He'll surprise me, he says.

Once when he telephoned, he told me Frik was doing well and working at a bank. He said Frik asks about me and would like to call me sometime.

"Thank you, Wouter," I said. "But I don't think that's a good idea."

From the Kids

Scottie sat on the front porch next to a big kettle with dry ice in it for Halloween the last year he was alive. He wore a costume and sat on a chair, still as night, with steam coming up from the ice. He didn't move a muscle until the Trick or Treaters got close to the door. Then he'd come up off that chair and ask them what they were doing at his house and scare them like crazy. They loved it. After Scott died, they reminisced in letters to Grant:

Remember the time I slept over at your house and your dad made us laugh our heads off?

God must have wanted someone really funny and really nice to talk to.

Remember when your dad scared me on Halloween with the cat that spun its head around and screamed?

I liked your dad because of the stuff he said. His last words to me were, Okay, Buddy!